SWEET SIREN

Those Notorious Americans, Book 3

CERISE DELAND

COPYRIGHT

W. J. Power Publisher

Photographic art: Romance Novel Covers

Graphic designer: Wicked Smart Designs

ISBN-13: 978-0-9908943-8-4 Digital

ISBN-13: 978-0-9908943-9-1 Print

❀ Created with Vellum

DEDICATION

For my husband Steve, my staunchest supporter for nearly five decades, my boundless love and appreciation. You have always been my hero!

For Susana Ellis, whom I have never met in person, but who continues to be my gracious co-hostess each Wednesday at 5 Eastern on Facebook for our party Teatime with Cerise and Susana, my gratitude. I certainly could not have done it every Wednesday without your support!

CONTENTS

FOREWORD

Money can buy anything, can't it? Those brash Americans--their dollars and charms work wonders. Until they learn that money can buy anything...but love.

WILD LILY, BOOK 1

DARING WIDOW, BOOK 2

SWEET SIREN, BOOK 3

SWEET SIREN

Tycoon. Robber baron. Builder of ships, dreams...and a fortune. Few women can resist him.
One tries.
But who wins when their choices are revenge—or love?

⚜

Killian Hanniford has everything he wants. Charming children, a growing empire and wealth beyond his hard-scrabble childhood dreams. He doesn't need a wife. Doesn't look for love from the women who only want to dip their hands in his wallet.

But one woman cuts him cold—and he wonders why she has the nerve.

Olivia Bereston knows the notorious American millionaire well. He's ruthless, unprincipled. And she's delighted to cut him down to size.

But afterward, he finds her amusing. Intriguing?

Is he mad?

Or is he so unique, so forgiving, she might even learn to forgive herself for her own failures? And love him for all his charms?

CHAPTER 1

October 1878
Saint-Paul-Saint-Louis Church, rue Saint-Antoine
Paris

Killian Hanniford stared at the priest. Focusing on Marianne, his niece, the bride, he tore his mind from the lady in the third row who had eluded him months ago—and given him the cut direct at another family wedding.

Waiting in the vestibule for his niece to arrive, he'd spied the woman as she arrived at the church with a girl who, by her resemblance, had to be her daughter. Surprised to see the lady again, he made no effort to hide his interest. He was called a blackguard, and by God, he could act like one. So he skewered her with hot eyes. She glanced away...but returned to lock her umber gaze on his. Proud, wickedly pleased he'd made her turn, he grinned at her like the scoundrel he'd been. She'd caught her breath and spun away, then hastened down the aisle.

He'd jangled her nerves. *Good.* He'd do more. Few people

ever insulted him. She'd done it in public. To say nothing of the fact that she was sin in motion. Tall, regal, with a crown of bright red hair, luscious pink lips and ripe breasts no corset should touch.

He inhaled, burning to have this ceremony end. To waylay her. Trap her. Not let her escape him. Not again. She'd answer for her pique. Answer to him. And he'd enjoy undoing her. Her black witch's eyes on him in the vestibule had told him she found him hellishly attractive.

Well, that makes us even, dear lady.

He snorted.

The priest glared at him. Then continued the marriage ceremony.

Killian smiled, counting all the fabricated reasons why women were attracted to him. Clear-eyed, he had no illusions about his so-called allure. First, foremost, he had money. Millions. Ridiculous wealth by American standards. A damned fortune by current European measures, considering the Irish upstart he was. He had friends, too. Bankers like the Rothschilds. Industrial leaders like the Frenchman Jean-Baptiste André Godin. Businessmen like John Garrett, president of the B&O Railroad in Baltimore. Painters like Renoir and Degas. The sculptor Remy and his bride-to-be, Killian's niece, Marianne. Noblemen like his son-in-law, the duke of Seton. If Killian also possessed moderate good looks and a healthy body, he called himself fortunate in that also. At forty-seven with another birthday next month, he still had a full head of black hair, albeit with a few strands of gray to add a distinguished mark to his poor Irish origins and his dastardly robber baron reputation.

When a woman approached him, Killian made it a rule to discern her motives quickly. Did she wish to dip her fingers into his pockets? Did she want a brief escapade, diamonds or a house for her trouble? Did she want the excitement of a longer affair with the man who could afford to buy and sell most British aristocrats and still live like a king?

For more than a decade as a widower, he'd enjoyed himself with women who'd desired each of those arrangements. He'd found not one woman who challenged him or understood his drive. He needed no mistress of his homes. He needed no heirs. He had a son and two daughters, plus a niece, all of whom he adored. His wife had died thirteen years ago. Loving her dearly as he had, he never intended to replace her. And when he used his wealth to expand his empire from Baltimore and New York, Texas and Connecticut to England and France, he found women everywhere eager to please him. Especially ones in need of funds. Ready to sell their bodies and their souls to get rights to his check book. In drawing rooms and gambling halls, at the opera and in restaurants, women of breeding and refinement flocked to him. He was never lonely. Never bored. Alone only when he wished to be.

So it struck him as bizarre—funny, really—that a woman who refused to permit an introduction to him should command his attention.

The Catholic priest cleared his throat.

Killian snapped to attention.

"Sir?" The man gave him the signal that he could place the hand of his niece Marianne into that of her soon-to-be husband, the duc de Remy.

Killian handed her over. He should be listening to their vows. Rejoicing in their union, the culmination of a stunning love affair begun in the Rue de la Paix in Paris on the same day that his oldest daughter Lily met her future husband, the love of her life.

But his duty done for Marianne, Killian stepped backward to the front row of chairs in the church. He sat wrestling back the urge to turn and meet the gaze of the woman who had dodged his reach. The hair at his nape bristled. Did she watch him? He smirked to himself. Of course she did. He filled with satisfaction that they might enjoy a mutual attraction. Certainly, she had lived in his thoughts for months. But he was no love-sick youth. No callow boy.

His oldest daughter swayed against his side.

With a steadying hand to her elbow, he glanced at her.

She gave him a shake of her head and a smile of small apology. Lily and her husband, Julian, had arrived from London on the train two days ago. She'd seemed pale then and though she'd gone to bed early each evening, even after their dinner party last night, she didn't seem much better this morning.

He frowned.

Marianne, his niece, had not looked any better. She, too, had seemed wan this morning. A bride might have nerves, but Marianne was not normally ill. Nor was Lily. And both young women looked decidedly unwell. Unsteady on their feet too.

He should be focused on them. Not the woman behind him.

Whatever her name is.

"We've not met," he had said to her the first time he'd laid eyes on her five months ago in London at Julian's sister's wedding breakfast. She'd caught his eye with her vibrant red hair, her radiant gown of blue moiré and a funny blue feathered toque. She caught his imagination with her exuberant smiles and animated conversation. From across the crowded room, she seemed alone, without a male escort, which pleased him the longer he looked at her.

When he made his way to her side, she looked surprised. Worse, affronted, as he said, "Allow me to introduce—"

"But I know who you are," she said in a rich voice that soothed like old brandy. Outrageously beautiful, she had an oval face, high cheekbones and delicate winged brows. Accenting her pearl-like complexion, she had dark chocolate eyes and an elegant bearing that spoke of breeding...and condescension.

"You have me at a disadvantage. Unfair." He took a flute of champagne from a footman and placed it in her gloved hand.

Her delicious looking mouth curved in a polite line as she accepted the glass and raised it to him. "We must keep it that way then."

Undaunted, he cocked a brow. "You have no name?"

"I have one that is immaterial to you."

He chose not to consider her response rude, but teased her. "How do you know?"

She chuckled. "Because we meet here only by chance. This once. Never again."

His eyes locked on hers. She denied him even the courtesy of introducing himself? *Scandalous*. Intriguing. "I could ask about. Learn your name. Your age. Your father's and grandfather's birthdate and—"

"My husband's too?"

That gave him pause. Married. He never stole other men's wives. Not even for one night. "I wish to compliment you on your wonderful laugh. I overheard you as you talked with that gentleman there."

"Thank you. I believe it's important to laugh fully, cry until you're sick...and to avoid dangerous men."

All humor had drained from her large fathomless eyes. Then, she'd put her glass to his for a brief click and had left him where he stood. Mesmerized.

The priest droned on with more of the Catholic wedding service.

Killian winced, focusing on how lovely his niece Marianne was in her pearl-encrusted gown that Monsieur Worth's staff had hurried to sew in three weeks' time.

Next to him, Lily leaned a bit toward her husband. "I'm sorry," she whispered to Julian who took her hand.

"Are you well?" Killian asked his daughter.

"Light-headed. My apologies, Papa."

The service required that they take the kneelers. "I think you should rest. Go straight back to Boulevard Haussmann and lie down."

"And miss Marianne's and Remy's wedding breakfast?" She stared at him as if he'd grown two heads. "Never."

He patted her arm.

To Killian's left, his younger daughter Ada leaned forward and arched her brows. "What's wrong with Lily?" she mouthed.

"Excitement," he offered.

Ada shot him one of her cat-ate-the-cream looks. "Pregnant."

Killian blinked. At eighteen, his youngest chick could be too precocious.

She rolled her eyes at him.

He winked at her. She had predicted this months ago, soon after Lily and Julian were married. Whenever this conception had occurred, he did not care for a date, only that his daughter and her child be healthy.

The organ music swelled and the congregation rose to their feet. The priest offered a few more words and Marianne and her new husband faced the one hundred assembled guests in the Church of St. Paul and St. Louis. His niece who had weathered the ravages of the civil war in Virginia and who had endured marriage to a petulant, irascible man, had remained a widow for too many years. Here in Paris, she'd found enchantment with a Frenchman who was a duke and a prince of the realm and above all, utterly devoted to her. Marianne—bright, blonde and thirty years old—beamed like a first-time bride at those in the congregation. Her husband

—exuberant and a breaker of all kinds of rules—swept her up into his arms and carried her down the aisle.

Grinning, Killian turned to watch them go.

And his eyes met those of the woman with no name.

She was laughing. That same melodic peel of joy that had caught him spellbound months ago lured him again.

She stopped. Her magnetic gaze flowed from his to his hair and his lips and back to dwell softly in his eyes.

Madam, whoever you are, you must not tempt me like this.

As if she'd heard him, she glanced away. Her lashes fluttered. Confusion had her regarding the newlyweds as they passed her. But once they were gone, she stole another glimpse of Killian.

He was ready for her. Their gazes held and delved.

Ah, my dear lady, this time you will not deter me from knowing you. Fascinations are, like your laughter, uncontrollable.

CHAPTER 2

S he should not have come to this wedding.

Standing to one side of the gilded drawing room of Remy's *palais* on the Rue di Rivoli, she sipped her champagne and studied Killian Hanniford standing before a white marble column. The sun beamed through the floor-to-ceiling windows, silhouetting his muscular physique against the golden walls and crystalline mirrors. In his formal attire of grey striped morning tuxedo and stark ivory shirt and waistcoat, he was a vision of stark masculine power.

What *had* she been thinking? That she could appear here, enjoy the festivities, the wedding, especially this reception and avoid Killian Hanniford? *After what I did the last time we met? If gossips are to be believed, he'll give me the cut direct. Or more likely, crush me with one hand.*

She downed a gulp of champagne.

Oh, I'm an idiot.

And a liar.

She bit her lower lip. *Be honest with yourself, Liv.* Hadn't she come specifically to see him once more?

"Mama, Marianne is so lovely. Remy has chosen well, don't you think?"

Her daughter Camille, soon to be fifteen, had begged to attend this wedding with her. To take one's sweet child out in to society was not done when she was not old enough to have debuted. But then, Camille would be different from other young ladies of her class and her age. Lovely with a riot of golden red hair and earthy dark eyes, Camille looked more like a bold poppy than a frilly white flower. She'd attract men with her dramatic looks, and make her way in the world while fending off their indecent proposals. She had education and charm, but no dowry to commend her. Indeed, even her pedigree was a mark against her. But by her nature, sunny and jubilant, she belied the calamitous pasts of her parents. From birth, Camille had been a happy soul. Burbling. Talkative. Eager to embrace life. Butterflies and puppies. Roses and books.

Liv enjoyed her. Applauded her. And in Camille's wish to attend Remy's wedding, Liv had decided last week she would indulge her.

She'd called upon Camille's headmistress, packed her up and taken her from her school near Brighton. Camille had been shocked nearly speechless, and Liv was certain the child would expire with joy yesterday before their train pulled into *Gare du Nord*. Everything about the journey had become an adventure for her darling daughter. The extraction from that hideous school. The announcement they were to attend their cousin Remy's wedding in Paris. The new gown Liv had ordered her dressmaker to fashion for Camille. The train trip. Paris itself, the city that shimmered and sparkled with delectable food and fine wine, vibrant music and art. And Killian Hanniford.

She spied him across the room, talking with a woman who looked familiar. Liv told herself not to care who it was or why he beamed down at the lady with that predatory smile. After all, she and Camille were here briefly. Liv was ready to depart at a moment's inclination. Nerves eating her alive, she'd been thrilled at the lack of a receiving line. She wished to have a glass of champagne, thank her hostess, wish the newlyweds great joy and depart.

"*Ma cherie*, Olivia, I am delighted you have traveled all this way to join us." The distinguished Duchess de Remy and Princess D'Aumale appeared at her side. "I know Remy will be thrilled to see you. And you must meet my new daughter-in-law."

"*Madame la Princesse*," Liv said with the French accent the Princess preferred and gave a curtsy to her distant cousin, "I am honored to have been invited." *And received. That is so rare among English society for me and my daughter.* "But I must tell you that I met the young duchess a few months ago in London when I attended the marriage of the duke of Seton's daughter to the Earl of Carbury. Marianne is lovely in face and spirit. I know she is a perfect match for our Andre."

"She gave him a merry run, but I do believe they are meant for each other. And Camille, how charming you are, *ma petite chou.*"

Liv's daughter curtsied to the elder lady. "I am honored, *Madame la Princesse*. I begged Mama to attend."

"Right you were, too, Camille. Your mother remains too cloistered. I meant to bring you out, Olivia."

"You succeeded, *Madame*."

"A lovely party, *Madame la Princesse*."

Liv froze. He'd come. His rough voice wrapped around her like a velvet vise. He seized the opportunity to appear at her side now that the princess spoke with her. In such company, especially with Camille here, how could she once more be rude to him?

She stared up at him. He was so tall, he hovered over her. Like a gargoyle. Or a dark angel.

"*Monsieur* Hanniford, it is nothing," the Princess said. "I'm glad you allowed me to host the reception."

"I see what you mean now," he said. "Your home is much larger than our drawing room in Boulevard Haussmann. Better able to hold all the guests."

"We have so many in Paris whom we must acknowledge. I must extend greetings to all I know when I see how happy my Remy is with the woman he adores." The lady tipped her head. She was *haute Parisien* society, a descendant of the dethroned Bourbons and the rascally Bonapartes. She fluttered her fan against the necklace of sapphires and diamonds that some said Napoleon had purchased for his second wife, the Austrian girl. Marianne today wore the pearls that the first emperor had indebted himself to buy for his beloved first wife Josephine. "Have you met *Monsieur* Hanniford, my dears?"

"Not formally," Liv answered attempting *politesse*, but the princess knew the reasons why introducing her was nothing she'd ever wanted. Still, no matter those hideous facts, Liv had to set a good example in society for Camille.

Hanniford, infamous rogue that he was, did not turn a hair. He bowed slightly, a mischievous smile curving those full lips.

The princess did the honors. "Lady Savage, may I present my daughter-in-law's uncle, *Monsieur* Killian Hanniford?"

There was nothing for it. Liv held out her hand.

He took her fingertips and bowed over her hand like a prince. "Lady Savage, I am delighted to meet you."

"Miss Camille Bereston is Lady Savage's daughter whom I am to understand persuaded her mother to take her from school just to witness Remy finally take a wife."

Camille held out her hand and Hanniford took it and sweetly shook it. "I am honored to meet you, Miss Bereston."

"And I you, sir. Mama says you are one a person must know."

Liv sucked in air.

"Did she?" His eyes seared Liv's with silver flames. "My reputation precedes me in far too many ways."

"Oh, sir, she said nothing derogatory about you."

The princess was smiling.

Liv felt her cheeks flame.

"I'm glad to hear it, Miss Bereston."

"Camille, *ma cherie*," said the princess, "I understand you and your mother will return to London tomorrow. Come talk with me, will you? I miss our discussions of novels. Forgive us, will you, Olivia, *Monsieur* Hanniford? I shall return Camille to you in a few minutes."

Liv agreed. Of course she did. What else could she do?

"The princess engineered that nicely," he said, his gaze following the lady and Camille, but turning back to her with a wicked smile.

Liv would not surrender to his charm. "She is very adept socially."

"One would believe it," he said, moving ever so slightly closer, engulfing her in his subtle bergamot cologne. "I am grateful."

She licked her lips.

He narrowed those incredible silver eyes on her. Piercing her with his intent, he said, "You've heard of me. What I do. Who I am. And you thought I was a monster. That's what Camille was referring to, wasn't she?"

"You do have a reputation, sir. Ruthless, indomitable."

"I am not always that. Especially not when I meet a lovely woman who—"

"Sir, this is not proper. I must go."

"Where is your husband, Lady Savage?"

How dare you ask that. "Not here."

"Clearly. Will he not come with you to social events?"

"You are bold, sir."

His silver eyes sparked with interest and no shame. "Is that why you stay away?"

"No." She pressed her hands together. *Could she not escape?*

Hanniford stepped closer. "Will he look kindly on you attending dinner alone here tonight?"

"Yes. No. Mister Hanniford, do stop."

"My lady," he said as he drew away, "I do not wish to alarm you. Forgive me."

Hanniford does not give in. Hanniford does not apologize. He presses. Demands.

Liv put a hand to her ribs. She had to stop remembering her father's words. "My husband is dead, Mister Hanniford."

His mouth dropped open. But satisfaction replaced his surprise. "My condolences."

"There is no need. He died six years ago. My daughter and I are accustomed. Forgive me, I must collect Camille."

"Stay, please."

Could he be pleading?

He touched her hand briefly. "Drink your champagne."

She stared up at him. She could live every day looking into his eyes that sparkled with apology.

"You look uncomfortable but if you drink your champagne, you'll appear more at ease. Besides," he said, his heavy masculine voice dropping to a silken whisper, "you'll relax. I won't bite."

She did take a sip. The alcohol whirled in her brain while she gave into the mesmerizing spell of his quicksilver gaze. "I must ask her how she knew to leave us alone together."

"Knew?" he asked, laughter playing at the corners of his eyes and lips.

13

Oh, curse the man.

"Easily, I'd say." He glanced over her shoulder, for all the world appearing nonchalant. "Your words to me are sharp. Lethal, even. But the way you look at me?"

She could not breathe. "Yes?"

"Says you cannot have enough."

She swallowed, forlorn, defeated. "A terrible mistake."

"Why?"

"I'm not anyone you should know."

"Why?"

She took another drink of her champagne.

"Lady Savage, I don't think your formal title suits you. I wish to call you by your given name. What is it?"

She sputtered in outrage. She had to put him in his place. But the imp inside her wanted to yell at him—or grin at him. "You cannot know what I am. Savage, kind, impertinent, sweet."

"But I'd like to."

Oh, had all her bravado deserted her? She shook back her curls, the wisps escaping her coiffure and distracting her. "I see now how you have earned your millions, Mister Hanniford."

"Do you?" He grew playful. His stance protective, proprietary. "And what is your assessment?"

"That one must be fast to outfox you."

"I'd like nothing more than the pleasure of your company." He inched ever closer.

Her spine stiffened. Her eyes widened. "Impossible."

Horrified, he stayed his ground. "I'm sorry. I've frightened you."

"No. That's what's remarkable. You're not frightening."

Irritated he saw her attraction to him, she lowered her armor. Like a silly debutante she wanted to be coy with him, not thrust and parry in a game she hated to play. She closed her eyes. Waved a hand. "Do all women fall at your feet? Do as you wish? Give you what you seek?"

Raising his face to the ceiling, he laughed heartily. "Well, ask my children. Ask my niece too, will you?"

She found herself beaming at him.

"That's more like it," he murmured. "I marvel at how beautiful you are when you're happy."

Foiled, she glanced at the wedding guests. How could he disarm her like that? "Sir, you must not."

"Admire you?"

"Stop."

"If I admire your laughter and your looks, I cannot help it, my lady."

"Olivia—" she corrected him and mentally kicked herself. She shouldn't humor him.

"Olivia." He rolled the name around his tongue as if it were a sweet meat. "I like it."

She beckoned a footman and she placed her empty glass on his tray. She was making a fool of herself, one minute arguing with him, the next eating up his compliments. "I really must go."

"Don't. Talk to me. The princess has not returned Camille to us yet. We have time."

"I should collect her."

He put a hand to her wrist. His long fingers were a warm solid band that set her pulse jumping. "I hope you will attend the Princess's supper party this evening. Do you?"

"No." Looking at his hold of her, she shook her head. She mustn't come, though she had packed dinner gowns. Three of them. For what? In hope that she'd feel comfortable in Paris? More comfortable here than in London society? Or that she would see this man. Want to be in the same room as this man. Why? To assault him with her accusations? Ridiculous. She was too polite, too worn by years of sadness, too devoid of that fire to confront him with her litany of woes.

She loved to dine, converse, and yes, laugh, but usually did not except with clients. Now that she'd seen Hanniford again, talked with him and dueled verbally with him, she understood why her father had warned her that she must never do that. *He can seduce you with a trick, a word, a grin.*

"We won't attend the supper tonight. My daughter and I return to London tomorrow."

"Must you go so soon?"

"I hadn't planned to stay long. Only enough to see Remy happily wed." *And yes, I shall admit it to myself, to see you again and reaffirm how handsome, how devilish, how fiendish you are.*

His brows knit. "I am in London often. I hope you'll permit me to call on you after I do arrive."

"Thank you, no." She would not wish to be so near to him again. Not wish to be lured from her old hatred of him. Not want him to see her humble house. Small, dark, spare as it was.

"Then I will invite you to dine with me. With other guests, of course. No one will think it amiss if you join me for a large gathering."

The scene flashed through her brain like golden rain. She'd relish the décor, the guests, the conversation. Him. *Oh, if only I could...*

"I like it when you smile at me," he said with a sincerity that had her grinning at him like a Mad Hatter. "Allow me to take you home."

"No."

"Obstinate woman," he bemoaned. "Then do promise me you will return here for supper tonight."

"I can't." *Mustn't. The temptation to seek you out would be too alluring.*

"All right. Instead I will bring dinner to you."

She laughed, long and hard. "No. You will not!"

"I'll take a private dining room at the Grand Hotel de la Paix. Have the chef in the Cafe send up five courses."

"Ridiculous!"

"Good! Tell me your hotel. I'll be there to fetch you at—"

"No, sir. Do not!" But she was chuckling, captivated by him.

He seized her hand and brought it to his lips, supple and enticing on her skin. This time he lingered and when at last he gazed into her eyes, she had no breath. "Dine with me, Olivia. I will show you I am no ogre, but a man of culture and honor."

"Do you attempt to charm all women with such eloquent declarations?" She tossed her head, loving the thrill of clashing with him—and flirting with him.

"Only you, Olivia. Only you."

"Thank you, sir. But do not continue. Excuse me, please." Her head high, her heart low, she left him where he stood.

CHAPTER 3

L iv managed a glance down the long dining table in the Remy Palais on the Rue di Rivoli. For more than two hours, she'd avoided looking at that particular spot where Killian Hanniford sat. In his black swallowtail tuxedo and starkly white cravat and red satin waistcoat, he'd captured her attention when first she entered the palace again tonight at eight. He'd greeted her with a heated smile and kind words that all could overhear. If she detected hints of undue interest, if she caught intimations of invitations to speak personally with him, she assured herself those were wishes. Unwise ones.

She concentrated on the glories she enjoyed of an evening in a glamorous home with famous people. Breathing such fine air was such a rarity that she was giddy with it. The food, the wine, the wit of the combined families of Hanniford, Seton and Remy filled her with a delight and a gratitude that she'd been invited—and that she'd decided to come.

Camille, as was her place for one not yet officially out, had not come for the formal soirée but remained at their hotel. That establishment tucked in the corner of Boulevard Saint-

Germain on the left bank was not among Paris' most elegant, but it was what Liv could afford. And it was safe. Respectable. She'd had no misgivings about leaving Camille alone in their small suite. And her daughter was happy to bid her good night.

"Remember everything, Mama. I will write about it in my newest novel."

Her daughter fancied herself a writer. Liv did not discourage her, either. Camille, like Liv, would have to find a means to earn a living. Her daughter knew her place in society, disgraced as she was by both her mother's and her father's names. And like Liv, her daughter predicted that should she marry, she should not depend upon a husband to support her. Or even if he did at first, he might lose any wealth he possessed. Just as her father had. And her grandfather.

"Shall we retire to the drawing room?" the Princess d'Aumale said and rose to her feet. "No need to split, do you think? I'd say we need cigars and brandy. All of us together, eh?"

Andre, the duc de Remy, laughed. Sitting at the left hand of his mother, he arched a brow at his new bride across from him, and said so all might hear, "Mama would like to enjoy a cheroot."

"I think she should," said Marianne with a wink at her mother-in-law.

"Will you join her?" Andre leaned forward to ask her.

"Not tonight. But I'll save my marker for a future date."

Andre waved a hand toward his guests. "On notice already, and I'm not married twelve hours yet!"

The party of sixteen, all family in one degree or another, got to their feet. Led by the Princess, Andre and Marianne, they filed out to the hall and drifted toward the drawing room or the ladies or gentlemen's retiring rooms.

As the throng thinned, Killian fell in beside Liv.

"I like the purple on you. It highlights the pink in your cheeks and the eloquence of your dark eyes."

Liv grinned and smoothed her long gloves over her elbows. "I like the red of your waistcoat. It reminds me what a rebel you are."

He laughed. "If you refer to my years running ships though the Union blockade, that was long ago."

"But it's how you gained your wealth."

As they strolled into the drawing room, he took her arm to lead her to a settee for two. "You know so much about me and I know very little about you."

Sitting beside him, her hip against his, she grew warm. She put a hand to her throat. She'd worn one of her best pieces, inexpensive silver. Cheap really. All the estate jewels gone to the auction houses decades ago.

His eyes followed.

Of course he could tell their worth or lack. But his gaze was too intimate to indicate he assessed the value. He appraised her. *Only her.* "Won't you tell me about yourself?"

Her mouth watered. Why did he unnerve her so? Because he was nothing she had anticipated. Ruthless, brusque and mean was how she had pictured him. But she'd witnessed him be only courteous and funny. Kind and unnervingly intuitive. "I would have thought in the interim, you'd ask Andre or the Princess about me."

He pursed his lips and considered the others who gathered in the room and took their places. "I prefer you tell me."

"Why?"

"You'll tell me the truth."

You would not appreciate it. I would hate it. So why would I even attempt it? She fought for some diplomatic exit. "Ah, but I could embellish the tale. Most people do when describing themselves."

"I doubt you'd do that with me."

She drew back, once more impressed with his insights. "You have faith in me but don't know me at all."

He sat back, one arm gliding along the back of the settee and creating the illusion that he embraced her. The heat of his body infused her. "I make it a practice to examine those I find intriguing."

Is that how you've gained your wealth? Your ruthless reputation? She fiddled with the sticks of her fan. "Oh? How, exactly?"

"I examine posture, breath. Even poise, eloquence. I read you during supper."

She had to counter him, didn't she? "And what did you learn?"

"You love being here. You were natural, born to this, but oddly sad."

That took the wind from her sails.

"I don't know why," he added in a bass murmur full of sorrow. "But I will learn."

"I don't wish it."

"If we are to continue, I will need to know how to make you happy."

"Continue?"

He nodded. "We will. I wish it. You do too."

She shook her head. "No."

"The way you look at me has changed since this morning's festivities."

She swallowed, trapped. "Please don't."

"But it has. Then you appeared curious."

A thrill ran up her spine. And fear ran down. "I will not ask how."

He looked triumphant. "Now you are hungry."

She snapped her fan together. *My God, this conversation was becoming outrageous. Torrid.*

"You've no need to panic."

"I'm not," she found it necessary to declare.

"No need to run, either."

Oh, hell. Why not be as blunt with him as he was with her? "I do not want to know you, sir. And you should not wish to know me any better."

"Both lies."

She met him, eye to eye. "I cannot believe you've succeeded in business by pursuing those who do not wish it."

"On the contrary, that is exactly what I've done." He leaned closer, his mouth an appealing slash. "And most were happy that they'd made my acquaintance."

I know one who had never said that.

The princess, Andre and Marianne were seated, the footmen passing round brandy and cigars, while the guests took up various stances or chairs.

"I think," said the princess as she nodded toward the grand piano, "we could do with entertainment. My dear, Olivia, would you do us the favor of your talents?"

Delighted to escape him, Liv gave no thought to refusing. She shot to her feet.

Hanniford was up beside her. "Shall I turn the pages for you, my lady?"

"No need. Thank you." She noted the surprise in his silver eyes. *Good. I need to stun you. Make you ignore me.*

"What shall it be?" Andre asked her.

Liv smiled at the newlyweds. "For you, my dear Andre and Marianne, a composition that speaks of all the delights of love."

"Wonderful," said Marianne, as she refused with a polite dismissal of her hand the footman's offer of a cigar.

Liv strode to the huge black piano. "I think Chopin."

Killian was at once beside her, pulling out the upholstered bench. "Please," he offered graciously.

And she sat.

Inhaling, she called upon the years in which she'd lost

herself in music. Years of lonely torment when sanity came only from the notes of passion that flowed from her fingertips to fill her childhood home and later her husband's. Only in the technical demands of countless hours of sonatas or etudes or little ditties she herself composed, did she find an escape and a means to cope with the innumerable failures of her father and her husband.

The audience grew quiet, rapt. To her left stood Killian Hanniford, hands clasped behind his back, at the ready should she ask for a score. But she needed none. Never had. Not for a decade or more. Bars of compelling notes danced in her head. She called on them when she needed inspiration for her work. Sonatas, particularly those by Chopin, were the pieces that flowed through her head when she designed the final elements of a drawing room, an orangerie or a bedchamber. Noblemen and aristocrats and the new American moguls like Killian Hanniford demanded extraordinary, monumental and above all, unique décor for their new country homes.

Chopin. Who loved, lost, and died too young and too full of regrets seemed a poignant choice for the evening. He embodied romanticism and above all, she was here to celebrate how love could enhance one's life...even if she did not believe it. Even if she'd never had any evidence of it. Nor ever would.

She put her hands to the keys, struck by her own paradox. She could not love. Not anyone other than Camille. She had lost. Lost her *entrée* to society and lost any desire to regain respectability. And as for regret, she'd vowed years ago never to waste her time regretting anything she could not change.

That cut Killian Hanniford out of her life entirely.

What then to do about that tiny corner of her heart where fondness for him had taken root tonight?

She hit the first chord and sat back, jarred by the discord. Once an evil flower had grown in her heart. She'd tended it, named it vengence and hated herself for it. In its place, a different plant sprang up. Regret rooted and blossomed.

Might she find it in her heart to enjoy his company? And if she did, could she ever forgive herself for her failure to shun him?

❦

Killian shook himself from his reverie. Olivia had given them Chopin's piano concerto Number 1 and he was unable to regain his equilibrium. He talked, he smiled, he refused brandy.

But he needed only to talk with her, smile at her, understand how she had become so accomplished as a pianist. Indeed, he'd heard many a great composer in London concert halls. Here in Paris, he'd been honored to hear many more. Never, in any drawing room, had he heard their equal. Until tonight. She stunned him.

He was astounded by her talents as a pianist. She had evoked such heartbreak and delight from the keys that his eyes stung with hot tears. No musician had ever done that to him. How could he possibly let her go without telling her how profoundly she affected him? Not only as a musician either.

But as a stirring, irrepressibly strong and vibrant woman.

And now, if he detected her movements clearly, he could see she was leaving, excusing herself from her hostess and Marianne and Remy. Other guests stood, presaging their own departures.

Killian had to do more than say goodbye to her.

"Andre, Marianne," he said as he reached their sides. "Forgive me. I will go too. It's been a long day. I'm sure you both could do with less company."

They laughed and looked at each other like conspirators.

"We could," Marianne told him and stood on tiptoe to kiss him on both cheeks. "But we've decided we're not going south tomorrow."

"That's a surprise," he said. Marianne had written to them that she wanted to spend her wedding trip in the south of France in Provence. "I thought you'd taken a house in Arles for two months."

"We cancelled it yesterday," Andre told him as he curled an arm around his bride's waist and kissed her on the crown of her head.

"I'm expecting a child, Uncle Killian. Can you believe it?"

"What? But...that's marvelous! That's why you look so pale." He shook Andre's hand and patted him on the back. He lowered his voice, and leaned close. "When did you learn?"

"Yesterday. I felt so fatigued. The doctor came and examined me. I can't believe it, Uncle Killian. I didn't think I was capable of it."

Andre hugged her near. "I told her I didn't care if it never happened. But it has. And believe me, I am thrilled. But I did want her to enjoy our wedding day more."

Marianne pinched her husband's arm. "I did! All of it. Especially you carrying me down the aisle as if I were your prize."

"You are! You will always be."

Killian turned aside as his daughter Lily and her husband Julian approached them.

"Good night, *Madame la Princesse, Madame la Duchesse, et Monsieur le duc*," Lily said with a flourish and kissed her cousin, then allowed Andre to kiss her on both cheeks. "Congratulations once more and thank you for a wonderful day, *Madame la Princesse*. We'll come visit you tomorrow before you both leave for Arles."

Marianne looked like the cat that ate the canary. "But we

were just telling your father that we're not going until next year."

"Why ever not?" Julian asked Andre. "I thought that was to be your wedding trip."

"It was. However, we now have a reason to remain here for many months."

"Oh?" Julian asked him. "A new commission for you?"

A broad smile played about Andre's face. "A new endeavor, *oui*. I am to be a father."

"So that's why Marianne looks so pale," Julian said with a grin and embraced his friend. "Congratulations!"

"Thank you. She hasn't been able to look at breakfast for weeks. She's been craving chocolate too. All odd. We should have known, but yesterday I called a physician and he arrived and confirmed it. Marianne is in shock, but laughing about it all!"

"Oh," said Lily with a blank expression on her face. "I never thought—"

"What?" asked Killian.

Lily stared at her husband. "I've missed...um...well. You know and I—"

"What?"

She sagged, looking stunned.

"What's the matter, darling?" Julian caught an arm around her back.

"I'm—I'm—" She put a hand to her forehead.

"Lily?" said Julian, Andre, Marianne and Killian as if in chorus.

"I'm pregnant, too."

"What?" Julian steadied her on her feet.

"I should have known," she said in a daze. "No breakfast. No food. The smell of beef made me ill."

Congratulations and laughter went all around.

"We have to get you back to Boulevard Haussmann,"

Julian said. "Come on. We won't be going home tomorrow either."

"Oh, but—"

"No, if you're not up to it, we'll be fine here in Paris."

"You will stay as long as you need to," said Killian.

"And do come for luncheon," said Andre. "All of you."

"Why not?" his mother asked. "You'll stay for a long restful time in Paris and dine with us tomorrow!"

Killian couldn't believe the news. Two new babies soon to be in the family. When he'd sailed for Europe last year with Lily and Marianne, he'd hoped they'd find men they loved and who valued them. He hadn't planned beyond that. Not for children. A grandchild. A grand-nephew or niece. He was fortunate. *Old.*

"What's this?" asked Olivia who made her way among them.

"We are to have two new babies in the family." Andre was chuckling.

"Marvelous news," Olivia said with a grin. "Babies are such fun."

Lily who leaned on her husband's arm, said, "Perhaps later they are. At the moment—"

"Oh, dear," said Olivia with sympathy. "I see you suffer with the early stages. I am sorry. But it passes. And then the joy of expectation is wonderful."

Killian admired her exuberance. Her delight at the idea of children. He wondered if she had more than Camille at home. Where was home? And where did she live?

She tugged on her gloves as Andre's butler presented her cape. *"Merci beaucoup* for a marvelous wedding and all the festivities. I've not had such a good time in years."

The Princess accepted her kisses on both cheeks and Andre embraced her. "You have not graced us as often as you should. I require you to return to us soon. Spring perhaps?

We are to have the choirmaster and the organist at the Basilica of Sante-Clotilde at the Opera. You will want to see them."

"I'd like to very much. Thank you, Andre. I will consider it. But well, you know I must consult my schedule."

"Of course. But you have an open invitation."

"I will remember. *Au-revoir*."

"Have you a carriage?" Andre asked her.

"No, I will hail one."

No carriage? Killian seized the chance. She could not walk about alone in Paris at night. "She rides with us, Andre."

At his words, Olivia stared at him. "I don't wish to impose."

Andre shook his head. "Let Killian do the honors, Olivia. I would feel better. And you will be safe."

She shot Killian a glance that said she did not believe that at all. But with Lily and Julian in the carriage, she had some safety.

"My cape, please," Killian told a footman. "Good night, *Madame*, Andre, Marianne."

Minutes later, he offered his arm to the lady who had refused him more times than any woman ever had. Behind them, Julian and Lily spoke in whispers of delight and concern as they descended the steps of the palace.

"You're very proud of yourself," Olivia said as he and she awaited the arrival of his carriage around the bend from the mews.

"I am. And you will be safely to your hotel."

She huffed.

"You don't believe it," he said with a chuckle.

"Why must you always win? You realize, it's very tiresome."

I don't always. "I can lose gracefully."

She lowered her chin and glowered at him.

His grin grew wider. "Shall I allow you a victory?"

She blew a gust of air. "I must claim more than one."

"Ah, but then you'd never see me again."

His coach pulled up, the footman opened the door and Olivia climbed the step inside. Killian sat next to her. Settled there in the ruby velvet squabs, the street lamps casting rays of light gently upon her elegant face, Olivia looked ethereal and more carefree than at any time today.

He brushed her skirts to one side and lowered his voice as Lily and Julian climbed into the large town carriage. "What if I offered you a bargain? One that was more than fair."

She stared at him, her expression saying she did not believe him.

"You would win in all but one thing."

She grabbed a breath. "I suppose to be sporting I'd have to agree."

"Want to hear it?"

She turned away, laughing. "Yes. Tell me."

"Whatever you want, it's yours. But in return, I must have two things only."

Lily settled into the opposite seat and her husband followed, sitting beside her. She sighed.

"I'm glad the evening was not much longer. I'm really quite exhausted."

Her husband cupped her face, brushing her cheek with his thumb. "We'll be home soon and then you'll go to bed to sleep as long as you want."

"Thank goodness," Lily breathed and put her head on her husband's shoulder, then shut her eyes.

Boulevard Haussmann was only a few minutes away from the Rue di Rivoli. Lily and Julian were out of the carriage quickly, bidding them good evening.

Killian told the coachman to wait a moment. "Where to, Olivia?"

She gave him the name of her hotel and they were off again in the enveloping silence of a crisp autumn Parisian night.

"You said, you must win in all but two things. Tell me," she said, her gaze fully in his, "What they are."

"The pleasure of your company."

She huffed. Considered her folded hands in her lap. "I don't think I've given you much pleasure."

"You could."

She stiffened her spine. "I can't imagine how."

"Laugh with me," he said. "Carefree, you are irresistible."

Her dark gaze melted into his. "I am not carefree. And I laugh infrequently."

"All the more reason for me to find ways to make you smile at me."

She gave a rueful shake of her head.

He tried for more. "Play Chopin for me."

She squeezed shut her eyes in denial.

How to win her over? "Dine with me."

"No."

"With others. Family. In public. A proper—"

"No."

That last was emphatic. Nigh unto vehement.

"Women generally don't challenge you." She arched her elegant brows, her marvelous dark eyes twinkling. "I am no mountain to be conquered."

"Most women want something from me. You want nothing from me and a part of you even dislikes me."

The raw honesty of his remark made her flinch. "I dislike you less every minute."

His fingers twitched. *Victory could be had here.* "Then I must extend the moments until you dislike me not at all."

She tossed her head and grinned.

"I want to enjoy your company. Have you not had any relationships with men based on that?"

"Never."

That told him he was right to pursue her. "Then now is the time."

"And you are that man?" she asked as if she considered it possible.

"Name what you want," he rushed to secure the deal. "Anything from me."

She took her time thinking on that, her mouth pursing, her gaze tracing his mouth. "I would not want our relationship to appear more than friendship."

I thought not. "Whatever we become to each other, no one would find fault."

"I would never ask for things that were...risqué."

More's the pity. "I have one condition."

"I should have expected a bargain." She clasped her hands in her lap and considered them a long moment. "What is it?"

"That you tell me the truth."

She sank into the squabs. Her manner careful. "And if I say yes, will I regret it?"

"Never."

Her lashes fluttered. "How do you know?"

"Because I will never ask anything of you that you do not wish to give."

She studied him. And if he were right to wager, he'd say she did not breathe. "We are agreed."

"What would you have first?" he asked her, his body mad with raging heat to have her in his lap, in his arms, in his bed. But at the pace they went, that would take eons. He'd be eighty or dead in his grave.

Her eyes twinkled. "Would you walk with me along the Seine?"

"Now?" He took her hand in his.

She grinned at the sight of their entwined fingers, then looked up at him. "Yes, provided that..."

"What?"

She got a devilish smile on her lips. "That you wouldn't take it as an invitation."

"Oh? To do what?"

"Kiss me."

Tempting woman. "I doubt I should."

"Exactly."

"A shame," he said, suppressing a laugh. "What else might be on your list?"

CHAPTER 4

T
he night was cool for late October in Paris. She pulled the collar of her cloak higher against the breezes off the river.

The moon shone, full and buttery as he walked beside her along the *quai*. He'd chosen a portion of the Seine where fili-greed black iron gas lamps illuminated the cobbles and he ordered his coachman to follow a few paces behind as they strolled along. He'd left his top hat and his gloves in his carriage and she had left her little evening purse upon the seat.

Killian had relinquished her hand once they'd alighted, though his nearness, enticing and fragrant of bergamot, clung to her consciousness. How many years had it been since a man had made such an impression on her? Ah, she knew. Since she was an ingénue naive, gullible and unable to discern character from appearance.

They walked along the water's edge, the sounds of the river lapping at the docks draining her anxiety of meeting this man and the shock of enjoying his company. If she could now continue to reconcile her previous hatred of him with her delight at his attentions, she might learn how to forgive what destruction she'd endured after his theft of her prospects and her happiness.

"How did you learn to play the piano so well?"

Struck that he should ask such a pertinent question about the origin of her wounds and her salve for them, she avoided looking at his all too handsome face. "Years, hours, days of devotion to it. Most young girls take lessons early and I used it as an escape. As a cure. Medication. Laudanum, if you will, for unhappiness."

"I'm sorry. I've touched a nerve and meant only to compliment you on your expertise. I enjoyed it thoroughly."

"Thank you." She could be gracious. "I'm glad you did."

"Chopin is a favorite of mine."

The American tycoon had culture? Of course. How could he survive here or in London without it?

"My wife liked his etudes. I prefer his sonatas."

Oh, give over, Liv. The man attempts to be engaging. "Did your wife play the piano?"

"She did. Not as well as you. Your talents reminded me of her. I thank you for that as I don't remember her often enough these days."

Manners would be a good thing to display here. "How many years have you been without her?"

"Nearly thirteen. With her, I learned how to put all my efforts into winning."

"She knew your strengths?"

"And my weaknesses. She wasn't shy about reminding me of them, either."

Liv laughed with him. "A proper partner does that."

"I was fortunate."

Liv could not say the same of her own—and she strolled onward. "The river is serene tonight. It splashes softly against the docks."

He kept pace. "You like the water?"

"Yes. I do," she said smiling. He knew when and how to change the subject to a more agreeable one. "The sound is like no other. Gentler than a bell. Sweeter than a chime. Oceans, rivers, streams, seas. I am free in water."

"Do you sail?" he asked in that mellow tone that defrosted more of her defenses against him.

"No. Do you?"

"I leave that to others."

"How can that be? You own shipping companies."

"I do. I've commanded a few smaller vessels in the sixties. But I always had an experienced assistant on board. I know more about how to make them efficient for trade. These days, I let others run them with my instructions. Do you like to sail?"

"I swim."

He laughed. "Are you any good?"

"The very best. My older brother who died young sadly, was a very proficient swimmer. My parents had a country house and on the grounds was a man-made lake. In summer months, I'd sneak out and go with him to swim. My father declared it indecent and it was. I refused, you see, to wear one of those hideous women's swimming outfits."

"The shirt and the bloomers?"

"Just so. Scratchy too. And I didn't bother to use our awful bathing machine to travel to the water's edge, either. I loved the excitement of just...well, jumping in."

"I don't blame you," he said. "Swimming is meant to save your life or enhance it. Best if you can enjoy both. I know. A man who commands a ship must be as able and ready to jump overboard as his seamen."

The very idea of Killian Hanniford stripped to the waist, bronzed and brave enough to cut through rough waves had her pulse pounding. "Did you have to? Often?"

"A few times, yes. When I was fourteen, my best friend fell overboard in Baltimore harbor. He hadn't yet learned how to swim well and I went in to collar him and take him to shore. A few times, I've been aboard when we've encountered hurricanes. Days before our civil war broke out, we foundered off the coast of Jamaica. We lost three crewmen."

"That's sad."

"It ended badly." He grimaced and looked away from her for a minute, then turned back with interest. "So I'm intrigued about your swims. If you didn't have an outfit, what did you wear?"

"Ah, well." She blushed and wondered if he could tell in the dark of night.

"Ha! You're bright red. So you must reveal all."

She relented. "I borrowed a pair of my brother's falls and cut off my chemise at the hips."

He roared in laughter. "I'm shocked your mother didn't lock you up and throw away the key."

"She might have tried, but she was ill." *Locked away in her mind.*

"I'm sorry."

She could not dismiss his sorrow. Had not her mother suffered because of him? "She'd been ill for many years."

"So then, I see that one thing we must do together is go swimming."

She looked at him askance. "Impossible."

"Why?" he asked with a grin.

"I don't have time."

"Never?"

"No. But worse, I still don't have a bathing costume."

"All the better. Neither do I."

She broke out in laughter with him. Then she turned and walked on, soothed and excited by his humor.

"Tell me about your daughter," Killian said and pierced

her reverie. "She is poised and very charming. How old is she?"

"Fourteen. But she's to celebrate a birthday in December when she will turn—I'm certain—forty-two. But she's as lovely inside as out."

"I'm sure you taught her that."

She met his quicksilver eyes. "No. Camille came full blown at birth, giving a sigh as if she were quite delighted with herself and the world. She continues in that vein, finding charm in the smallest of things."

"You encourage her in that, I bet." He frowned at her. "Children do not continue with a love of life unless they have a good example."

"I'm afraid it was her father who led the way on that one. If he was excessive in his addictions and suffered for them, Camille has learned from that poor example to temper her tendencies to excess."

She stopped. Why had she revealed so much of David's faults? Honesty was one thing, but to disclose so much of her husband's sorrows was too damning. She put a hand to her brow. "I'm sorry. That was...unnecessary."

"But honest," he said with a tone of nonchalance.

She nodded. She'd promised him truth and he got it.

"Has Camille enjoyed Paris?"

Liv inhaled, appreciative of Killian's turn to another subject. "She did. Every girl loves a wedding, a romance, and when it is her famous cousin, the sculptor Remy, marrying an American heiress, she can talk of nothing but love and those who must live happily ever after. You see, she fancies herself an author of gothic romances—and I must say, since I've read a few of hers, she's good at it. So coming to Paris gives her fuel for her fires."

"Why not stay longer?"

"I must return to London."

"Duty?"

"Business." *Lack of money.* She hurried on. "I love Paris. So different from London and British society. My mother brought me a few times when I was a girl. Now I come for only a few days at a time. To complete my clients' orders. And my visits are necessarily short. But Paris has changed so much lately for the good. I don't know it well."

"When were you here last for a holiday?"

"Eight years ago. Just before the war with the Prussians and the terrible siege of the Commune. Andre's mother, the princess, was a godsend to many during that awful time. She fed the orphans, saving hundreds of them. She still does."

"I didn't know that," he said. "She doesn't speak about it."

"She wouldn't. Though she's richer by far than many, she uses her money to improve the city."

"That's what wealth is intended to do," he said with a conviction that had her questioning her previous assumptions of him.

She halted, surprised and intrigued by his praise. "You believe that?"

"I do." He examined her for a long minute, then shook his head. "You thought I was a fiend who created wealth to horde it?"

She tipped her head. "I know few who believe otherwise."

He snorted. "You haven't met the right people."

"I should meet more like you." *Though I think you are one of a kind.*

"That or get to know me better."

"To that I have agreed, good sir." *Good heavens, was she being coy with him?*

He grinned. "You mentioned clients. Are any of them trolls who horde money?"

"A few." She rolled her eyes. "After they part with much

of it somewhat reluctantly I might add, to feather their nests."

"And you help them with this 'feathering'?"

"I do. Tomorrow morning, I have an appointment with the manager of the *Sèvres* factory."

"The makers of porcelain?"

"Yes. I acquire the best in the world for the richest in the world. I commission complete table services for my clients. Often times, the design is original to them. Their motto or their crest baked in."

He arched a brow, in feigned humor. "You consult others on their dinner plates?"

"On their dining rooms, their furniture, their draperies," she said, loving that she astonished him. She stopped at a statue of some military man whose pose resembled that of Napoleon in Canova's infamous portrait. Hand tucked in his buttoned coat, the soldier had donned the same placid expression as his emperor. She admired this living man before her, this new emperor of industry, so much more handsome than either the French leader or his follower. "I consult most often with one architect on the construction of his clients new homes."

"Is that profitable?"

"For me? I daresay I am building a reputation for it."

"And increasing your fee as your prestige grows?"

She wrinkled her nose. "Why not?"

He lifted his chin, his profile strong and straight and true. "Spoken like a shrewd business person."

She waved a hand. "I'll take that compliment from a man who is termed shrewd."

He snorted. "Shrewd on a good day. Ruthless on all others. Am I right?"

He was. But she would not say that and once more be rude to him. "Perhaps they do not know you well."

"Or know me too well," he murmured. "And of your clients, have you any Americans?"

"I do."

"Would I be a potential client?"

Her heart hammered. "Many men now seek to cement their status in society by building homes that rival the aristocrats."

He looked out to one of the flat-bottomed *bateaux* as it serenely sailed past them. The wind picked up and ruffled a shock of his midnight hair, making him appear impossibly young and debonair. "I've contemplated doing that very thing. I've looked at plots of land, but found nothing yet that speaks to me of home."

Most men purchased land in a heat. On a whim. For cheap. Or to impress. Killian Hanniford, Irish immigrant, self-made millionaire, blockade runner and robber baron, wanted land that spoke to him of home and hearth. Admiration for him flooded her veins—and the part of her that shunned the scoundrel in him sat quiet, stunned.

She walked a few steps away from him, irritated with herself, trying to recover her composure. "Do you plan to stay in Europe for long periods?"

"I do."

Thrills of delight that she might see him often ran up her spine. "Then you might do well to plan a house. Land sells for a penny. Many like your son-in-law have inherited terrible problems from their fathers who were poor stewards of their estates. They're in debt to their eyeballs and cannot get out. They must sell any unentailed land or any asset that might bring them cash."

"That I well know. Julian has had to sell some of his assets to make ends meet. My financial adviser here in Paris tells me of two estates in England up for sale. I hesitate to buy them, though."

She had thought him unprincipled. How many ways could he disabuse her of that idea? "Why is that? If I may ask?"

"If I've been painted as 'ruthless', with my daughter married to a duke and my niece married to a prince and leader of the artistic community, I do not wish to continue that portrait. To buy land for a low price would endear me to no one."

Dear god. He has ethics even on the price of land? "True. But do consider, in your case, you're poised to change your own rank and perception. The purchase of the late duke of Seton's shares in his railroad did put you high on the social register in England. And I understand you negotiate with the Parisian Rothschilds to construct chemical plants in the north near Amiens."

He paused before her, his gaze probing and intimate. "You know a lot about me. How is that?"

She shrugged as if to indicate her knowledge of him was to be expected. But she had followed his achievements for years in newspapers. "You are a new element in our universe. Your businesses, your past, your family and future are all detailed in the papers. Killian Hanniford, former Confederate blockade runner turned industry titan. Father to three equally daring children and a charming niece. One of 'those notorious Americans' who've come abroad to sweep all vestige of the past away and create new worlds with your money and your optimism."

He scowled at the gently flowing river. "You really do have a poor opinion of me."

She would not lie to him.

"Come now. I hear it in your words."

"Yes, you're right. I did have a negative opinion. But...it changes." *God help me.*

"For the better, I hope."

"What you should hear is my applause for your boldness

and your skills." That was true. He was aggressive. That she did revere. She'd known so few men who had the courage to name what they wanted and found the means to take it. She huddled into her cape to cut the wind and to find warmth when she had been too honest and turned their conversation chilly. "I apologize. I do not mean to be combative."

"You've spoken your mind. I like that."

"You must deal with some very irreverent businessmen if you think my conversation has been kind. You've been a gentleman and I've been rather a witch. I'm embarrassed and sorry."

"Don't be."

"You're gallant, too. Meanwhile, I dislike my own bad manners and prefer being proud of myself." She took a few steps toward his coach. "Perhaps we should climb into your carriage and end the night."

"We can. First, agree to swim with me in England."

"*What?* No." She giggled at how he turned the tables on her. But then, she rather liked the idea of swimming with him. Where? "Oh, all right. When?"

"When I return to London in December."

"December? So will this be an ice bath?"

He donned a rogue's grin and undid her good sense. "Dine with me in December. Swim with me in May."

She struggled with a grin. "If you're hoping I'll wear cotton drawers and a muslin chemise, you are very mistaken."

"A man can dream. Besides, we're becoming friends." He stepped close to her, the moonlight limning his hair and his rugged complexion. "Wear what pleases you."

What would please her would be to wear absolutely nothing. How many years had it been since she wanted a sexual encounter? The very idea had been leeched out of her by the limited circumstances of her marriage. *Dear heavens.* She should leave. Avoid him. "That would be dangerous."

"I'm up to the challenge."

Dare she succumb to his charm? "Mister Hanniford, must you tame all the animals who nip at you?"

He cupped her cheek, his fingers drifting back ever so gently into the hair above her ear. "I try."

She gave a little laugh, but flowed more securely into his large hand. His palm was warm and moved, full of fond regard. How could he be so sweet, so tempting when the only trait she'd ever heard of him was his utter disregard for others?

"You now have a dilemma," he said to her in a gruff voice that fueled the fires of her desire for him.

She closed her eyes as he stroked the corner of her mouth with his thumb. "Which is?"

"Open your eyes, Olivia."

"Liv."

"Liv," he said her name like a prayer. "You must choose."

"What?" she asked as he wrapped one massive arm around her and nestled her against the bulwark of his body.

"To kiss me or not."

"And if I don't?" she said, her voice a hollow wreck.

"We will be friends," he told her as he put his thumb to the center of her lower lip and rolled it down.

"And if I do?" Her breath gone, her mind followed.

"We will be good friends."

She clutched him close. Desire was new to her. Passion a glittering land she'd never explored. "You tempt me."

"I know." His silver eyes flashed in the gas light. "What will you do with all that temptation?"

Seize it. She rose on her toes and brushed her lips on his. Could heaven be this tender, wild and mad?

"Liv, look at me."

"No. I'd rather do this." She slanted her lips across his and drifted into enchantment. This was what she craved. Him. She pulled away, her gaze on his, shocked.

"Liv," he beseeched her, "come kiss me again."

A ravenous sound escaped her and she kissed him with all the need he inspired in her. She held him tightly, fighting to encompass the massive strength that denoted his personality and his power. She broke away.

But he dragged her back and she kissed him with hunger. His tongue invaded her mouth and she allowed the heady claim. Bending her over his arm, he groaned and took the lead to kiss her once and then again. She managed a hand around his nape, his thick satin hair clutched in her fingers. His kisses grew demanding, wild. Her responses raw and needy.

He broke away with a start and she nestled her face into the wealth of his heavy wool cape. She heard him swallow hard and gasp for air.

This kind of affection was so new to her, so foreign. This was the stuff of a young girl's dreams. Or romances such as Camille wrote. About a man's kisses and embraces, the yearning for more, never to end. Naive, baseless fantasies. None of them realistic.

He put his lips to her forehead. "I'd like to kiss you again, but I doubt I'd live beyond the moment."

She pressed against him, words escaping her. What madness was this to want her arch-enemy with such ardor? She'd lived nearly half her life decrying who he was, how he lived, what he did and here she stood, in his fast embrace, caring only that he kiss her again and give her more of himself?

He stepped backward, his hands cupping her shoulders steadying her. On his face stood compassion like she'd never known. Desire like she'd never seen.

That too was unbelievable. A childish dream. Not meant for a woman of thirty-seven.

He glanced at the sky and bent to sweep her up into his arms.

She laughed, one arm around his shoulders. "Hanniford, you are a scoundrel."

He kissed her cheek. "But you like me."

God forgive me. "I do."

"Now," he said as he made his way along the *quai* toward his coach, "I call that a good day's work."

CHAPTER 5

Boulevard Haussmann
Paris

Julian walked into the breakfast room the next morning just as Killian was finishing his coffee.

"You seem chipper," Julian said, smiling at Killian as he strolled to the sideboard and picked up a plate. "Enjoyed yourself last night with Lady Savage, I gather."

An understatement. Her wild kisses. Her surrender. Her laugh. Her humor. Her eloquence at the piano to render the compositions of Chopin. Killian liked nearly everything about her. Except the puzzling reason why she initially evaded him and with such antipathy, too. "I did. She's intriguing."

Julian surveyed the dishes, uncovering one tureen and then another. "She's a bit of a mystery to us all. Seems a good sort."

"Fine company." Killian didn't intend to break his vow that his relationship with her be unremarkable in the eyes of society. His family as well.

"I liked her too. Last night was the most time I've ever spent in her company, even though she's a distant relative of my mother's. And of Remy's family, too."

"I don't recall her attending yours and Lily's wedding."

"I believe an engagement of some urgency prevented her." Julian closed the domed lid on a tureen and strolled to the table to sit next to him. "She works, I think."

Killian wondered what Julian might share about Liv. "She told me she consults on house decoration."

"Is that so? Well, good for her. My cousin, Lord Burnett, knows her much better than I."

"Burnett?" The name was familiar.

"Mmm. John? John Arden? Tall, jovial chap. You met him last month at our house in London. Perhaps at my father's funeral too."

Killian eyed the black band on Julian's sleeve, the one indication of his mourning period for his deceased father.

"Yes. The one who wanted the Winterhalter portrait of his mother?" The man had desired only one item from the estate of Julian's father, the previous duke of Seton. When that man died in June, his will granted the valuable painting to his nephew, the baron.

"Yes. To hang in his well-appointed twelfth century castle."

"I vaguely recall him." He tucked away the information for future reference.

"His mother was friends with Liv's mother, I do believe." Julian took a bite of his poached egg. "I did understand she got a very small widow's portion when her husband died. His house, land, goods were all entailed. Went to his relative, next in line. You know how that goes."

"I do." Killian had concluded she lived modestly. She had told him her husband had passed away six years ago. When he'd accompanied her home last night, he'd assessed the

Parisian hotel she stayed in while here. The Hotel Saint-Germaine was respectable, clean, quiet, middle class. What she could afford, then. Whether business called or not, she'd told him as they parted last night that she planned to return to London today after she finished her appointment on the outskirts of Paris at the Sèvres factory.

Killian had tried to persuade her to remain in Paris, but she refused. Then he'd pressed her to promise to allow him to call on her in London.

"I must think it over," she'd said and he couldn't get her to relent.

He'd circled his arms around her in his carriage. Tipping up her chin, he'd said, "You might need more kisses."

The pained expression on her face had been one of pure torture. But she'd said, "Good night, Killian."

And what he heard was, Good bye.

Panic raced through him. He wanted to argue, negotiate. But he didn't.

Delicacy was the better approach. He'd ask about. Find her home. Her business. Attraction such as they shared was no passing fancy. No infatuation.

He lifted his coffee cup and drank, eager to change the subject to a more positive one. He wanted more information about his daughter's health and her new revelations. "You seem well rested. Sleep well? Both of you?"

"That we did. Rather, Lily did." The grin on Julian's face could not have been more jolly as he paused to reflect on his pending parenthood. "Thank god. As for me, I sat watching her most of the night. Thinking. Money. Estate. The future."

Killian arched a brow at him. "You'll be fine. Everyone is. One grows into fatherhood. But I must say, I'm surprised Lily only just realized her condition once she heard Marianne speak of hers."

"I agree. Lily is so knowledgeable about physical conditions and maladies. You'd think she'd be constantly aware of how she feels. But what can I say? I know my tenants benefit from her care." He paused to stare at Killian. "I suppose not all women have sickness in the morning. Lily hasn't. Though she has complained lately of fatigue."

"You won't let her overdo herself now, I hope."

Julian shook his head. "She'll stay in bed, if that's what suits her. I don't want her traipsing about the tenants' cottages, either. I'll get Lily to hire a proper nurse for the estate. Lily can train her to her satisfaction. We'll pay her well and she can go down and treat them."

"A fine idea," Killian said.

"Lily's, really. When she was so tired last week, she suggested it. I liked the idea then. I love it now." He picked up his coffee cup and drank. "I hope you don't mind if we stay a few days."

"Absolutely not. Remain as long as you like."

"Good. The train was fine, but she wasn't keen on the speed. Looked a little green, actually. I should have thought of all this then."

"Don't criticize yourself, Julian. We men don't tend to think of our wives getting pregnant, until they are and then we fall all over ourselves ensuring their safety and their comfort."

"I'm going to insist she do less," Julian said.

"A good idea." Killian had loved pampering his Aileen when she'd been with child. Four times she'd blossomed, queasy only in the first few months. Never a problem delivering until that last one in 'sixty-five when she and the baby died of a prolonged and agonizing labor. After she'd gone, he scoured his memory for any little comfort he might have missed giving her. His grief was a ravenous animal that had eaten him alive for more years than he cared to count. No woman had meant as much to him since her passing. Lust was a shallow thrill, minutes long. Desire, though, was an emotion he'd long forgotten. Olivia Bereston awakened it in him. He welcomed the joy in it, even if he was shocked that at his age he might feel the buoyancy. Infatuation was more the word for her lure for him.

"What do you think? Killian?"

He faced his son-in-law. He had Liv on his brain. "I'm sorry. What did you ask?"

"What to do for a woman who is carrying a child? What do you recommend? I'd ask my mother but you know that relationship was never worth a farthing."

"Ah. Yes. Well. Lots of rest. She should eat whatever she wishes. No riding a horse. Any idea how far along her pregnancy might be?"

"Dear god." Julian stared at him with a wrinkled brow. "I didn't ask her what she estimates. She wasn't in the mood to talk at all last night. She's still surprised. So I can't say what a date would be. I mean, well...hmmm...she might have conceived right after we were married in June, but then that would make her..."

"Four months along," Pierce strolled in and grinned at Julian. "She wouldn't still be nauseous. Or would she?" He glanced at his father.

"I don't think so. Women react differently during their term. My wife was a shrew for the first child, sick as a puppy for the first months of the second, and fit as one of my Baltimore dock hands during the third. But you're the best judge of timing, Julian."

"Quite so," he said, lost in thought.

"There was that journey Lily took to Ireland in August," Pierce reminded them as he picked up tongs to select his breakfast sausage. His tone was all too casual, as the family did not speak of that period when Lily had left her husband. "So?"

"Yes," said Julian slowly. "Ireland."

How long had Lily been away from her new husband? Killian still had no idea and didn't wish to embarrass his son-in-law by bringing up what was a delicate subject. His daughter had left her new husband two months after their wedding and without notice, traveled to Ireland. Killian had not asked all the details. Many of them were none of his business and while he could be a demanding bugger, he would not meddle in his children's marriages. Or anyone's. That led to catastrophe.

Julian frowned at his plate. "She might be three months along...or more than one."

"Ask her later today when she feels up to talking. She should be able to count the months she missed."

"Oh, right. Of course." Julian went back to his breakfast.

Pierce took a seat next to his father, but focused on Julian. "How is Elanna?"

Killian inhaled. He didn't care for Pierce's continued interest in Julian's sister. The twenty-year-old young woman had married a much older man, the earl of Carbury, three weeks after Lily and Julian had wed. A beauty with rosewood brown hair and hazel eyes, she was a spitfire too, who had turned like day to night upon the occasion of her betrothal. At the same time, Carbury, too, had become more taciturn and more sinister. When Julian's father, the previous duke of Seton, had suffered a stroke during the wedding breakfast and died in the parlor, Elanna and Carbury had left immediately after the burial. Carbury, demanding and secretive, had insisted that he take his bride on a wedding journey. She had not argued, but in fact, sneered at her mother, the dowager duchess, and happily made a path to the front door and the Carbury carriage. Elanna had raged like a child at her fate. And for some unfathomable reason, Pierce was attracted to her.

Killian had always been proud of the fact that his son was

wise in the matter of women. Pierce was twenty-six, a shrewd businessman, two inches taller than Killian, fit, handsome as hell with raven hair and tender dove grey eyes. He had no mistress. Never had. If he'd taken women for a night or more, he didn't keep them longer. Wise in that, he was also selective in the young women he paid any court to. None at home in Baltimore, New York or Boston had caught his eye. He never spoke of any of them, never sought any information about them. Not as he did Julian's sister.

That worried Killian. Greatly. Elanna was a gently reared lady, daughter of a duke, now sister to one. Worthy, or so would say the aristocrats, to marry an earl. And she had. Everyone knew she'd married because the duchy was nigh unto bankrupt. All the Hannifords knew this because the marriage negotiations for Lily's dowry and annual income had been a nasty battle. But after her betrothal, Elanna had turned bitter. Resentful that she'd been turned out, forced to marry a man she disliked. And that put it mildly. She'd come to hate her status so much and begun to hate her husband so intently, that she was lost to herself. Resentful, angry and outrageously self-centered, she'd become a harpy. Few wanted to be near her. She sequestered herself at home in the countryside. There, according to letters Lily wrote to him, Elanna spent lavish sums on new gowns, furniture and a massive glass hot house conservatory. She also drank to excess and smoked tobacco.

Julian looked morose. "She's not well. Still belligerent to me. Does not receive my mother. But then, I don't either, so that's no problem there for me. I have received Carbury once. Last week."

"Oh?" Pierce took a bite of bacon, his grey eyes sharp as daggers. "What did the old bastard want?"

"Asked me to invite the two of them to dinner."

"Why?"

"She won't speak to him. He's worried."

Pierce picked up his coffee cup and drank.

Killian watched him. Pierce clenched his jaw, his face so yearning, his anger so raw he grew red in the face.

Julian put down his fork and knife. "I might as well tell you. Lily knows. Elanna is expecting."

Pierce blanched. "The bastard."

Julian winced. "Carbury called the doctor when she had a screaming fit two weeks ago and fainted."

Pierce's cup hit the saucer with a crack. "Christ. He torments her."

Killian knew from watching the Carburys together that that could be true. Carbury had a way of putting himself in front of Elanna at every turn. He interrupted her conversations to correct her. He advised her on her attire. She would sneer at him or laugh. That irritated the man all the more. They were both to blame.

Julian cut a glance at Pierce. "I think they do a fine job of tormenting each other. But he does want her to become more calm. He thought coming to dinner with us at Willowreach might have a good effect on her."

"But you and Lily haven't been there. Are you going down to Kent?" Killian asked.

"No. Lily wasn't feeling up to it and I'm up to my neck in the harvest. The loss of my estate manager has been a blow to me. I'm having to learn quickly what's to be done and done efficiently. I won't let my tenants starve this winter."

"Good man," said Killian.

"Last year, they did without hams and turkeys, vegetables too. I read it in the books. My father was scrimping on everything he could. I won't. I need them and I want them healthy."

Killian nodded, remembering the discussion he and Olivia

had had about noblemen who could not order their estates to be profitable.

"In any case," Julian went on, sitting back, "Elanna will have to learn to take care of herself. If she's not happy with Carbury, then she must attempt to discuss her problems with him. Not scream or throw things at him. And now there's a child coming into this. She must change."

"Carbury, too," Pierce added.

"Carbury, too," Julian agreed.

The three ate their breakfast in silence for a few minutes.

Foster, his butler, entered and presented Killian with an envelope on a silver tray. "*Monsieur* Hanniford" in fine script was upon the front. On the back, the crest of the hotel to which he had delivered Liv last night after the most stirring kisses he'd enjoyed in years. It bore no postage, so the item must have been hand-delivered.

"Foster, who brought this?"

"A coachman, sir, from a public carriage."

Killian shot to his feet. "Just now?"

"Yes, sir."

Killian threw down his napkin and bounded for the foyer, the front door, the steps, the walk. He halted in the road. At the far corner, he spied a black carriage, one of those public hackneys with a worn shiny top. It was rounding the circle.

She'd gone. Too far to catch. But she must have decided to stay in Paris. Meet him for dinner or the theater.

Heart pounding like a boy, he grinned and tore open the missive.

> *"Dear Mr. Hanniford,*
> *Last night was an idyll. I shall not forget it.*
> *But we will not continue.*
> *With regards,*
> *Lady S."*

❧❧

She dare not look back. If she did, she'd return. And she mustn't.

"What is the problem, Mama?" Camille asked her, her sweet chocolate eyes sad with concern as she bent toward her in the cab.

Tears clogged her throat. She crushed her handkerchief in her lap.

"What did you just do?"

Liv put two fingers to her mouth and willed herself to calmness. "I thanked Mister Hanniford for his kindnesses to see me home last night."

Camille studied her for far too long. "After you returned last night, you were awake for a very long time."

Cursing myself for my weakness in liking him.

"I wondered if perhaps he'd..."

Liv stared at her daughter.

"Kissed you."

"No."

Camille laughed and clapped her hands. "He did! You're blushing!"

"Don't, Camille. Please." Liv glanced away, wishing the oil cloth in the window were clearer so that she could view the bustle of people in the streets.

"And you're sad. Why?"

"Stop this."

"No. Mama, is he that much of a scoundrel, a—a what do they call these Americans? A buccaneer? So bold that you cannot allow him to be your friend?"

"He does have a scurrilous reputation." *And I was taught at a young age to hate him.*

"Tell me about him."

What little information would suffice? With Camille,

there was not room to guess. "Much of what Mister Hanniford has done is to build his businesses."

Camille put on a tolerant face. The child was too precocious. "Mama, that is not an explanation."

"He had dealings with your grandfather. Years ago during the civil war in America. Mister Hanniford owned ships that transported cotton for the southern states to England. He charged exorbitant rates for his goods."

"But your father didn't sell goods. He owned his own ships."

"Mister Hanniford earned great wealth and bought out the shares of my father's shipping company."

"So this is how grandpapa lost his business?"

Liv nodded. "It is."

"So you dislike Mister Hanniford for that."

"I hold him accountable for his actions, yes."

"I see. Was the price fair?"

Liv squared her jaw. "Not the price my father asked."

Camille turned her face to her own window, her brow furrowing. "But grandpapa had other businesses. The coal mines. And wasn't he invested in a train? With the old duke of Seton? Julian's father?"

"He was allied with him, yes. Seton bought him out for a pittance." Another bad bit of bargaining on the part of her father. Liv bit her lip. She hadn't meant to share that last. But Camille was a smart girl, capturing everything said in her presence and everything unsaid as well. Family secrets were difficult to contain with such a wizard in her midst.

"Does that have anything to do with Mister Hanniford?"

"What? The purchase by Seton of your grandfather's shares in the train? No, nothing." *But it was part of a series of challenges from which my father did not recover.*

"This purchase of your father's shipping line happened how many years ago? In eighteen-sixty?"

"Sixty-one." Liv frowned. Camille knew foreign affairs, too. She was well versed in reasons for the great recession that had occurred in England because of cotton shortages in the mills. Liv could not avoid expanding her knowledge. "Eighteen years ago."

"Isn't that a long time to hold a grudge?"

Liv squeezed her eyes shut and swallowed the sharp words she wished to scream so the world would hear. "Your grandfather's financial failures had long term effects."

"So much so that after all these years, you cannot enjoy Mister Hanniford's company?"

"Yes. Some hardships are not forgotten." Lack of food. Lack of money. The fear for tomorrow. The disgrace. A mother crazed. A father stunned and stoic. "Some failures are not easy to dismiss."

"Even if you like someone—"

"Even if you do."

CHAPTER 6

April 1879
Brighton, Sussex

Killian paced the length of his private car as the train chugged toward Brighton. He should have come south months ago. But the land agent he wished to see had been ill and only recently recovered. That delayed his plans and his hopes for a quick start to construction.

English weather was hideously unpredictable and to get a finished product within the normal ten-to-fourteen months construction period, he should have begun building last month. This month, at latest. To add one need upon another, he should be at Willowreach. His oldest daughter Lily was soon to deliver her first child at her estate, while in Paris, his niece Marianne prepared to welcome her own baby.

"You're wearing a hole in the carpet, Father." Pierce motioned for him to reclaim his seat opposite him. "You said this man couldn't meet us sooner. What's his name again?"

"Gerald Carruthers." Killian had been surprised that his

son, who made friends fast and wide wherever he went in Europe, had not met this agent.

"Ah, yes, Carruthers. Works only in Brighton, I assume?" When Killian tipped his head, Pierce inhaled. "Well, there's nothing for it but to decide on this quickly and get back to Willowreach."

Killian saw the strain on his son's face. Pierce was concerned not only for his sister, Lily, but also for his cousin Marianne as their time approached. But he had another interest near Willowreach. Inexplicably, for a dashing man with mad dark looks who could attract any young woman he wished, he was drawn to Lily's husband's married sister, Elanna, the Countess of Carbury. He was worried sick about her. She too was at full term with her own pregnancy but she'd been outrageously angry about her condition, taunting her husband with threats of leaving him after the birth of her baby. Everyone in the family was on edge that she'd actually do it—and that the hot-headed earl would do something vicious to stop her.

His son was becoming everything Killian had hoped for. Sharp-witted, shrewd, quick to act on instincts that he'd honed the past few years, Pierce was already a millionaire in his own right. Soon, he'd sign an agreement in Paris that would earn him four or five times his current income. But this focus on Elanna would bring him only pain. The young woman seemed to specialize in it. And why Pierce thought he might be her savior, why he fancied the idea he might alleviate her suffering or change her Killian could not fathom. But Pierce's focus on her could only lead to disaster for both of them.

I must stop brooding about him. It gains me nothing. Him, either. Talking to him failed. In fact, no amount of persuasion could induce Pierce to end his infatuation with the woman.

"I agree," he said to his son. "We'll do this quickly today. Not worry about things we can't change."

Pierce cocked his head. "To fret is not like you. Is it all the babies you worry over or is this property here in town so tempting that you don't yet know how to negotiate it?"

Killian paused, his son too wise about his behavior to give him peace. Yes, he was bedeviled. Three pregnant women approaching their delivery dates. Birthing could be perilous, even life-threatening to woman and child. *And then there is that other matter. One other woman in particular who refused to see me time and time again. And I've no clue why.*

"No, I won't have tea with you, Mister Hanniford," Liv had refused him only yesterday as he stood before her on the corner of South Moulton Street near Hanover Square. She wore a gold wool cape that set off the coopery highlights of her hair and the sadness in her chocolate brown eyes. It was her fourth refusal in as many months to any of his invitations. This one she gave in person, sadly, while the others had been notes, responses to his written invitations addressed to her modest residence in Earl's Court. "Please don't ask me again."

He'd been undeterred. "I think I deserve a reason, Liv."

Her eyes flashed dark fire as she tried to appear polite. "I cannot walk with you. Ride with you. Dine with you."

"Do you warn me off because there is a gentleman who preoccupies your social life?" He ventured to be bold and intrude on personal issues.

"No. None." She tipped her head to examine him, her gaze narrowed and suspicious. "Why not ask about town to learn that?"

"Because I hoped you'd tell me," he said with a solemnity.

Her beautiful eyes widened as if—as if that was a shocking revelation. "Then how do you know where I live?"

"A business associate told me. It was in the course of a discussion of decorators and—"

"I see. You wouldn't ask but someone just told you."

"Yes." He stepped nearer to her and the fragrance of jasmine rose to send a thrill down his spine. Part of her anger sounded like fear. Of what? That she'd find him amusing? He grinned. That he would wager on with ridiculously good odds in his favor. "If there's no one special, then I see no reason why you cannot enjoy yourself for a few hours in my company."

She'd flowed closer, discretion in her posture, sorrow in her eyes but resolve in her words. "We are not suited."

"The way you kissed me says otherwise."

"Don't, Killian." That last was a plea.

And he knew then whatever her conflict with him, she struggled with it. He'd give her reasons to accept him. "I like Chopin. You render it so well. I like the water. You find peace when you're near it. I like talking with you, walking with you—"

She put a hand to her mouth. Tears glistened in her eyes.

"I especially enjoy kissing you."

"It matters not." She bit her lower lip, shook her head and marched around him toward the Square.

He let her go, watching her stride away with speed. He'd learned quite by accident that she had a business relationship with his architect. He hadn't asked about town. Hadn't had to. He'd simply walked into Antram's office one morning last December to discuss details of their contract and Roger mentioned that his most popular decorator was Lady Savage, Olivia Bereston.

Figuring the gods smiled on his hopes to construct a country house suitable to his rising fortunes in Europe, Killian had done what any potential client did. He asked for a description of her experience. Little in the way of personal information came from his inquiry and Killian had not broached that subject. For the past four months, he'd visited

Roger's office once a week for scheduled meetings regarding his new home and estate. While nothing definitive could be decided until he purchased land he liked, he relished the idea he might accidentally see her at Antram's offices. That had not happened until yesterday. And now the memory of her torment plagued him.

Why did she refuse him? Kisses as delectable as those they'd shared were not ordinary. To reject the truth of their attraction defied every instinct in his Celtic soul. Chances were she would kiss him again like that and when she did, they would explore more deeply than their mouths. Her fear told him she knew it.

"Father? You are not listening to me."

"You're right." He reached to take down his greatcoat from the rack. It would be cold as hell by the ocean today. When last he'd seen this property in February, snow had frozen on his nose and eyelashes. He liked the odd serenity of snow falling on water and wondered if Liv did, too.

"It's not like you to be distracted."

Killian agreed. "With grandchildren about to fill my days, I've much to think about." Besides, Pierce would think him a blithering idiot if he told him all the reasons why they'd come to Brighton. "You make me smile."

"Well, aside from the fact that you're changing the subject, that's good because you haven't really smiled in months. Tell me what I've done to cause it and I'll do it again."

Killian shook his head, weary of his internal conflict about his intended actions in town today. "You know me so well."

"Thank God I do or I never would have learned how to finagle a good price out of anyone!" Pierce crossed one leg over the other and brushed his hand down his thigh. He wore a dove grey wool suit that matched his eyes and contrasted with his raven hair. He appeared to be exactly what he was, decisive, dangerous and rich as Midas. "Won't you give me a hint of what we're about here today?"

For this trip, Killian had requested he come along but told him only that he wished his advice. "The agent I'm meeting sells this land for a family."

Pierce picked up his bowler hat from the seat next to him and smoothed the brim. "I see. You're not usually inclined to show interest in the landed gentry or their holdings. Why meet this one?"

Pierce loved land. In the past six months, he'd become insatiable in its acquisition. As prices fell from the bad harvests and import of American corn and South American beef, the aristocracy were shedding their holdings like water off ducks. Pierce saw the opportunities. He bought and sold what he liked and did it in thousands of acres. Killian often joked that soon his son would own more of England than the Crown. Pierce would chuckle, but had never denied it.

While Killian applauded any venture Pierce wished to put his hand to, he questioned if owning so much of England would bring Pierce any satisfaction. Last year, Pierce had invested in Paris public works. Water works, to be precise. When the new water reservoir and sewer systems were finished in the French capital in two years, Pierce estimated he would earn more than a million francs each year for more than fifteen.

But what he was doing in England was a different story. Pierce was buying farm land. Yet he wasn't a farmer. He wasn't a miner. He was, however, devoting more and more of his time to managing what he purchased. With a new cadre of personnel whom he hired as his estate managers, Pierce trained his staff to do his bidding. His emphasis was to improve the crops and update the agricultural methods like rotation that worked well in the States. But more and more of his advice focused on efficient use of tools and fertilizer.

Farming had never interested Killian, but then his children each showed signs of interest in subjects which had never been his priority.

Nursing and medicine for Lily, the Duchess of Seton. Painting for his niece Marianne, the Princess d'Aumale and Duchess de Remy. For his youngest daughter, Ada, flirting with every eligible man in Great Britain fully absorbed her. But Pierce had two fascinations. Agriculture. And Elanna, the reckless Countess of Carbury, who did not seem to know Pierce existed.

Odd, how your children turn out.

Killian bent to look out the train window. They were slowing, coming into the station in the seacoast town.

"Will you tell me our goal before we get to your appointment or am I to guess?"

Killian fished his watch from his waistcoat pocket. "Always on time."

Pierce sighed. "I give up."

"I suppose you'll learn soon enough." *My need of a house. A proper country house.* "I'm hoping to buy land here along the coast."

Pierce's bright eyes twinkled. "Here? You don't say? But I thought you liked that cottage in Ashford near Lily and Julian's Willowreach."

"I may buy it as well."

"Splendid. I like an adventure, especially one so unusual as Black Killian Hanniford spending his millions like a drunken sailor."

"Come now." Killian tugged on his overcoat. "I'm not that daft." *Am I?*

"You're different lately. That I can say. For now though

give me details on what we're about to see, please, so that I don't look like the idiot son in front of this man."

"I've learned of a project begun but abandoned for a crescent of townhouses up for bid five miles east of Brighton." *And a smaller parcel ten miles away.* "Another plot east of Hove."

"Townhouses? That's not like you to show interest in home development. And Hove? That little town outside Brighton? It's insignificant."

"Very soon, it won't be. The population of Brighton has doubled in the past forty years since the trains began running from London."

Pierce frowned. "The area along the south coast has not prospered since the early part of this century when the Prince of Wales built the Royal Pavilion. Queen Victoria prefers Osborne House to the seaside and she even sold the Pavilion, contents and all, to the Brighton City fathers."

"But the English, like Americans, favor seaside vacations for health benefits. The town will continue to grow. I'm sure of it. I want a piece of that growth. You might too, so I hoped you'd look at these and give me your assessment."

"Father, you know what I'm interested in. City development. Country estates with rich land gone bankrupt."

"You're a good judge of a bargain, Pierce. Besides, every town does need new housing."

"You've never been interested in building houses." Pierce scrutinized him. "Why now?"

Since I concluded it's the only way to get Olivia Bereston to talk to me. "Variety in investments is a good idea. You have said the same. I ask you to hold your conclusions until you see the property and hear my general plan."

Gerald Carruthers was a genial sort, tried and true English-man, rotund, pink-cheeked and jolly. "Now this land is offered for sale by a different owner than the plot of half finished townhouses," the man informed Pierce. Killian had learned who the owner was months ago. "Eager to sell, he is."

Killian placed his hands on the ledge of the medieval ruins facing the sea. The stones, once part of a Dominican monastery, surrounded an earthen terrace framing the blue waters where the Atlantic Ocean met the English Channel. Ivy and lichen climbed the old stones. Protected from the winds off the coast, wild flowers sprouted at the base around his feet.

Inhaling the briny sea air, he leaned out to sea and recalled the morning he and his sister had climbed aboard a rickety ship in the port of Waterford. Colleen had enough money for their passage, saved from her barmaid wages in the local pub. With their father and mother gone the year before, she sought to buy a better life for herself and Killian. And she had. Their accommodations had been steerage, a spare berth in a damp and moldy ship, packed to the gills with other Irish in rags eager to change their futures.

"I say, Father," Pierce said, shaking his head, "why would you want this parcel? Ten acres is too small to build any town-house crescent. Aside from this view of the ocean, it adjoins only craggy farmland. Not even fit for sheep, I'd say."

"I wouldn't want this as a development property. I like the view. The air. The seclusion. Especially this—" He pointed to the four eight-foot-tall arches.

"They're remains of a twelfth century monastery," Carruthers said with pride. "Some say a few Knights Templar hid here in the fourteen hundreds when they were chased from France by one of their kings. Brought gold with them and buried it on the grounds. Many a man has dug here about but no one's ever found it."

"Intriguing bit," Pierce said, though Killian smiled that his son was unimpressed by the lure of easy money. "Unusual, Father. But what do you mean to do with it?"

"Improve it." Killian strode along the rough-hewn granite arches. Cluttered with seaweed and errant weeds, the glossy rocks could do with pruning. "Landscaping to clear the detritus. Level it. Place flagstones and create a terrace to sit and contemplate the water."

Pierce snorted. "I do believe you're turning mellow on me."

Or senile.

Gerald Carruthers laughed politely. "It's a stunning site, for fair."

"Who owns the land?" Pierce asked.

Killian laughed to himself. *Caught.*

"The Savage estate," Carruthers said.

"Is that so?" Pierce asked with a sideways glance at Killian and crossed his arms. "I've met Lord Savage in town. He's done the rounds of banks, I hear. In search of liens against his estate."

"The young lord," Carruthers said with careful diplomacy, "does indeed seek ready cash."

"This plot is not entailed?" Pierce pursued the line of logic. "He can sell this legally?"

"He can," Carruthers said with certainty. "When he inherited six years ago, it's my understanding, the Savage estate was already indebted. Poor land management."

"Aren't they all that way," Pierce mourned. Then he walked around Killian and faced him. "You like this because it's on the coast?"

"I do."

Pierce inhaled and turned in a complete circle to view the environs. "Hmm. It's secluded now, but civilization may encroach. Why not buy that acreage there as well?" He pointed toward the land to the west and the stony beach, empty save for one elderly fisherman who struggled to haul his small rig ashore.

Killian contemplated the man, his boat, the future of this enterprise. It mattered how he bought what he wanted. Learning over decades that intentions were one means to please the universe, he knew methods were as vital to the success of a venture. He'd failed himself and others at one endeavor because he'd not been careful to attend to the ethics of it or the details. "What do you know about that gentleman, Carruthers?"

"Old Dunwoody's in his seventies. Any sum you offered him would be princely."

"Does he live nearby?" Killian asked as he surveyed the downs north from the beach.

"He has a cottage behind that hillock there." Carruthers pointed to the northeast. "He fishes every morning, eats his fill but sells most of his catch to the monger in Brighton."

"Family?"

"Wife and sons long dead, sir."

"So fishing is his life," Killian concluded remembering a hoary fisherman in Waterford who lived to ride the waves and bring in whelks and mussels, sole and crab. Silent as the tomb, but kept to himself, happy in his lot.

"You'd say so, yes, sir. Not soft in the head yet, though. A talker. Happy to weave the local legends. Especially of the Savages."

"Does he? Well, good for him." Killian said, fighting the urge to ask about the owners. Killian directed his next question to the agent but locked his gaze on Pierce. "What would be a proper price to offer him?"

"Two hundred eighty pounds, sir."

"Double it," Killian said as Pierce grinned in disbelief.

"And tell him we want him to remain in his house and to fish at will."

Carruthers blinked. "And—and you want this parcel, too?"

In truth, it was the first time he'd glimpsed it last month that he'd made up his mind. The sea was too strong a pull to deny...as well as that other factor of the owner and the previous ones. "I do. Make an offer to Lord Savage. Eight hundred is his asking price?"

Carruthers was up on his toes, bouncing with delight at his sale. "It is, sir."

"Offer ten."

Pierce blew air from his mouth and plopped his hat on his head.

As they strolled down the hillside, Pierce caught up with him. "No bargain, that land."

"I wasn't looking for one."

"What are you in search of?"

The answer that popped into his mind was not one he was ready to admit to anyone. After decades of acting only after research and deliberation, Killian was not one to bet on an unsure proposition. But he'd give Pierce an answer that would satisfy them both until he was at peace with the probability that he might do the impossible. He might fail.

He glanced at Pierce and looked away lest his son see more than he should. "A home."

CHAPTER 7

May 1879
No. 10 South Moulton Street
London

L iv re-read the last paragraph of the contract for the decoration of the seaside home to ensure she hadn't misinterpreted anything. The venture seemed too good to be true. To help Roger Antram design the interiors of twenty-four townhouses in Hove and one palatial country home west of it, she'd be fully employed for the next two years. Perhaps three. She'd buy a few new gowns and better yet, afford to take Camille out of that hideous boarding school and send her to a better one. Better than that, she'd earn more than she had in the past two years. A bright prospect when she'd lived so many years without any.

More than all of that, though, she itched to fill this client's new country house of twenty-eight rooms overlooking the southern waters with the most ethereal treasures she could conjure in her mind. Her mouth watered. The setting— the essence of it—was the finest she'd seen on any English coastline. Every ounce of her blood, every beat of her heart turned toward the view she knew so well. She transform the site into the most serene home in Britain.

But she shouldn't rush to do it. Mustn't without knowing who this potential client was. That worried her, having worked with one very cantankerous old gentleman two years ago.

She ran a fingertip across one of the lines in the contract. "I see, Roger, that you expect this house to contain all the latest improvements. Electricity. How many homes have installed it? Two in England? Bathrooms with running water, efficient w.c.s. Astonishing. We'll need the finest plumbers. And four lifts. Who does that? No one. If I decide to work on this, I may become as famous as you to have drawn the plans."

"We'll have work for years to come, Liv." Roger grinned. She'd worked with him on many houses over the past decade And on another country house in Norfolk last year. The client, a lord known for his penny-pinching ways, was the very devil to work with. Always late with his payments, too. "I'm happy with this client. He pays well and has already put down a deposit on my services and yours. I'm happy to post it into your account as soon as you sign that."

Oh, she was tempted to sign, then run out in the street and sing. But she refrained from such exuberance until she had the funds in her name. "For such largesse, what does he ask in return?"

"That you consult closely with him on fabrics, colors, appointments. He likes painting, sculpture too, and he has a growing collection of art from the impressionists. He wants it showcased here. He also asks for original art in the foyer. *Trompe l'oeil.*"

"Painting on plaster for depth perception takes a special artist."

"That it does and I assured him you knew of a few. One in particular."

She did. A very talented but very temperamental creature.

"Does he like cherubs and gladiators?" she joked, questioning now if she wanted to work with such an exacting client as this one seemed to be.

"I doubt that." Roger shook his gray head. "He's above such mundane concepts."

"I should like to meet him."

"You can. Simply sign." Roger pointed to the bottom of the page.

Looking up at Roger Antram, she arched her brows. She'd worked with him on so many different estates. "This seems in order."

"It is. Our legal team has reviewed it."

Leaning forward in her chair, she placed the papers down on the architect's desk. The sites were west of Brighton in Hove. Attractive, delightful to her in all seasons of the year. The fee was a fifteen percent increase in her usual amount per home. That, too, was wise given the extra responsibilities she'd have of choosing wainscoting, paint colors, marble, kitchen appointments and fixtures and so much more for two large projects. She'd also have to lease a house in Brighton while she worked on the last phases of decoration. "I have one problem, Roger."

Perhaps to learn who had bought this land for the country house, she could have a chat with the current Lord Savage. He was her husband David's younger distant cousin who'd inherited the title and lands from him, a *roué* so careless with money that he needed to sell this marvelous parcel. Why, after so many years of holding on to this, did he decide to sell now? She'd told him often enough that she wished to buy it, if she ever earned enough. That was not in her cards. Never had been, really. Now someone had come along and purchased the plot. Blithe chance and serendipity meant she was to design the interior of the home for the new owner. Odd, how ironic life could be. And mysterious. "You know what I mean."

Roger tipped his head to one side, sheepish. "I do."

She sat back, her palms up. "How can I sign this if I do not know who the client is?"

He removed his glasses, put them to the mahogany expanse and pinched the bridge of his nose. "It's the client's wish."

"Why?" The prickle of suspicion that rose up her back had her shifting in her chair.

"I wanted you to see how favorable it was to you."

She canted her head. "Before you tell me who this is?"

He walked toward his window.

"You're being terribly mysterious, Roger. I can't say as it's comforting. You and I have had a very good working relationship for many years now. Why change your methods of working with me? If I've been remiss, not done a client's bidding, then you must tell me what it is that I—"

He spun, one hand up to stop her. "Nothing, Liv. You've done nothing. Your work has been more than satisfactory. Exemplary."

She flung out a hand toward the contract on his desktop. "Then let's be done with this. Just tell me who this client is."

Willowreach
Duke of Seton's estate
Kent

She alighted from the coach, hesitating only a step at the sight of the grand old home of the dukes of Seton. Once when she was ten, her mother had brought her here for a family gathering. The current duke, Julian Ash, had been a baby, perhaps only two or three years old. The event had died in her memory, but the house lived on. The house was an ageless combination of Tudor, Stuart and Palladian styles. The first sight a visitor had on entry was its pink marble foyer and the grand staircase where portraits of centuries of noted Setons marched up the walls.

She took a deep breath. Picking up her reticule, she strode to the front door and knocked. She hadn't sent word of her coming. She hadn't wanted to alert anyone to her intentions, but Roger had told her that his client—and hers—was in residence at Willowreach as he awaited the birth of his first grandchild. So she'd come. Quickly. And with ripe intent to tell him precisely what she thought of his offer.

The butler opened the door to her and with polite efficiency took her name and that of the man she wished to see. "Might I also invite you to leave your reticule here in the foyer, Lady Savage?"

"You may," she said and surrendered it, along with her coat and gloves.

"Do follow me, my lady," he said and ushered her into the purple sitting room where she tried to focus upon a landscape painting of Setons at the hunt.

She examined the Ming and Ch'ing vases, then took up residence in a sumptuous red damask Chippendale chair before the butler reappeared. "Please come with me, my lady."

She followed him as he led her up the grand circular staircase to the next floor. Along the wide corridor he walked and opened the double doors to a large and well-stocked library. The walls and shelves were dark oak and the tall Palladian windows were swathed in vermilion silk draperies. It was a sumptuous room, comforting and quiet.

"Lady Savage, for you, Mister Hanniford."

She'd last seen him—was it ten days ago?—at the crowded corner of Moulton Street on a busy afternoon. In bright May sunshine, he had smiled down at her, his gaze as smoldering as a swashbuckling pirate. His black hair had shown like exquisite Japanese lacquer. His lips had spoken words so alluring that she'd recalled the lush sexuality of his kisses and the strength of his embrace. In her heart, she'd smiled at him as warmth swirled through her at the virile power of him. Then, she'd had to argue with him.

As she did now.

"I'm pleased to welcome you, my lady. Thank you, Perkins. Please bring us tea," and so Killian Hanniford dismissed the family butler. His gaze danced with silver fires but his demeanor was businesslike until the butler shut the doors. "Do come and sit with me, Liv. I'm delighted to see you."

She sailed forward to plant herself firmly before him. He stood with a large tome in his hand, some volume he'd take from the wall-to-wall shelves. Dressed in grey wool trousers, white linen shirt and sky blue silk waistcoat, he was informal and had not donned a coat to greet her. Indeed, she sensed he had not worn one into the library. Well, what did it matter if he would not stand on ceremony? She wouldn't.

"Mister Hanniford, you know why I'm here."

"To continue this discussion, I had better be Killian. And as for why you are here, I hope I know." He extended a hand toward two chairs either side of the large ruby marble fireplace.

"I won't sit."

"I hope you would. I'm certain your journey was long and I'm sure you came via public coach so that—"

She pressed her lips together. "I did."

He threw her a sharp glance. "So that was uncomfortable. Allow me to make you more comfortable."

Given his generous financial offer for the work he proposed, she had to frown at the double entendre. "I think you've done very well."

He narrowed his gaze, a question there. "Yet from your tone, I fear I must improve."

"Such as they are, your conditions are satisfactory." Infuriating man. He would not get the better of her. Declare how things were to be without her having any say. "I have my own set of conditions."

"Ah, good." He walked around her, a smile—damn him—playing at his marvelous mouth. "I thought you might."

She blew air through her teeth. The man was most irritating. "I'm quite serious."

"So am I." He sat and put out a hand toward the opposite chair. "Please. Until you do, I will talk of nothing."

She marched over and perched on the edge of one chair. Hands in her lap, she willed herself to stone. "I've read the contract."

He looked her over, his perusal tingling her flesh as his gaze passed her lips, her breasts, her hands and lingered over each again as he returned to dwell on her eyes. "I assume because you are here and you know it is I who hires you, you have signed it."

"I have."

He relaxed backward in his chair. "Tell me what you want."

"I need you to know I dislike the means by which you had me sign. Your anonymity was unprincipled."

He had the integrity to look guilty. "Given the numerous times you've rebuffed me, I imagined few other means to influence you to work for me."

"I accept your praise, your wish to have me work with you on your houses, but I don't approve of skullduggery."

"I don't approve of mine, either. You have a stellar reputation, madam. I would not hire you because you refuse my company."

She stared at him.

"Nor would I hire you to induce you to share my company."

His frankness insulted her as much as it soothed her. "Thank you."

"You're welcome."

"But I won't be manipulated on anything else." She had to demand that of him.

"Such as?" His face grew stern, the lines of his jaw firm, his eyes steel. This was the robber baron. This was the blockade runner. The brutal negotiator, infamous. Ruthless.

"I use the best materials. I demand excellence from plasterers and plumbers, the stone cutters and even the painters. Once you see the selections I've offered you and you have chosen and approved, you will not meddle."

He pursed his lips, examining her minutely. "I believe in allowing the experts to do their work as they see fit."

She'd advised on many a house design outside and in. Yet no one had ever termed her an expert. The word complimented. It also implied excellence. "It is what I demand."

"I'm honored that you would still come to require it of me," he said with less ferocity in his manner.

She hooted in laughter. His change of tone could drive her to climb the wall. "You shouldn't be."

"Still...you have the look of a woman who has stepped into the lion's den."

She snorted. "If I were in my right mind, I wouldn't be here."

"But you are," he said with delight in his voice. "Tell me why."

She sucked in air.

Humor twitched about his mouth. "If you come here to

berate me for manipulating you, the least I can expect in return is your honesty."

That I rejoice at the chance to be near you. That I will not want more. That I want minutes in which I can dream of your lips on mine and wish— She shook herself. "I want this contract. The work is exciting. All the latest home improvements. I want to be a part of that."

Pride gleamed in his marvelous silver gaze. "I'm glad."

"But there is more."

"Continue then."

"The twenty-four townhouses were originally planned in the eighteen-thirties. While the foundation remained dormant and the plot of land undeveloped, the houses erected around it are fronted of gault brick. The look is very antiquated. The town council constantly criticizes them for their staid appearance. So I wish to recommend a livelier style of red brick and half timbered gables."

"If Roger agrees with you, so do I."

She cocked her head.

"You thought I'd argue with you?" His luscious mouth spread with amusement.

"I did."

He lifted a shoulder. "Anything else?"

"Yes." She rushed to her next consideration before she was disarmed by his agreeable nature. "The foundations are solid cement blocks and cannot be re-arranged without great expense."

"True. Did you want to make each house bigger?"

"No. But gas and plumbing specifications have changed and much improved in the past fifty years. I want your assurances that you will permit Roger and his staff to design the newest."

He nodded. "Electrical equipment, as well, yes."

"And that you will hire a local Sussex builder whom he recommends."

"I will not stand on my prerogative. I want the best. That's why I've hired Roger and you." He lifted those long dark impressive brows. "How else to gain top price for the sale?"

"Precisely." He would think that, wouldn't he? He was Black-hearted Killian, wasn't he? Her father had been right. So right to name him that. "If I am to work on both projects simultaneously, I must live in Brighton. But also I must travel to suppliers in London and Paris."

"You're right. I hadn't thought of travel."

She stuck out her chin. "I must have a living expense in addition to my fee."

"I agree. What would you consider appropriate?"

"One hundred pounds a month."

"One-twenty."

She bristled. He could not buy her. "I don't need that. One hundred will do."

"Then I shall add the twenty per month to Camille's school fees. Let the headmistress deduct it from her tuition."

She could not argue with that. More fool she, she welcomed it. "You make this very difficult for me."

"I hope to make it all very easy for you," he rejoined.

"Killian..." Oh, she was mistaken to call him by his given name.

He beamed at her. That familiarity broke innumerable barriers and allowed for too much intimacy to flow between them.

"I want this work, Killian. Both the townhouses and the separate home."

"Good. I thought you might find the challenge attractive."

"The house on the cliff is to be yours, isn't it?" she asked, unable to ban the wistfulness from her voice.

He nodded. "I've looked for a setting that spoke to me. This does. Like you, I find the sight and sound of water soothes my soul. You are the best person to create the right tone there."

"You must consult with me," she said because she wanted his perspective, his preferences to form the core of her work for him. She was doing exactly what she'd do for any other client. Even as she realized it would put her in close contact with him on far too many occasions. "You will have to tell me what you like. What pleases you. Not only colors, fabrics but furniture that excites you or soothes you."

"I will. But I must say, on much, I will only state what I like and leave the implementation to you. There is one aspect of the private plot that I must have exactly as I envision it. I enjoy the stone windows to the sea. I will not have them changed."

She met his stirring silver gaze and thrilled to his reference. "The old monastery arches? Oh, I agree. No changes to them. They are incomparable, aren't they?"

"So you've seen them and remember them?"

"Yes, yes. Decades ago. When I was a child and we visited. I played there. There is a tale that the Knights Templar buried gold florins from the French king's treasury up on the hillside. As children, David and I used to dig in search of them."

"David?"

"My husband. I knew him...or rather our families knew each other. We played together up there beneath the arches. I cannot imagine how they've withstood the test of time and storm and sea."

"Nor I," he said in a reverent whisper. "I want them preserved. Shored up. The wild flower banks along the path to them improved. The terrace connected somehow to the house. I don't care how you do it. Just give me that."

"I will. Never fear. I love them too. It's as if they've stood this long as sentinels to the centuries. As if they've proclaimed they can endure. As if they challenge what we build to last as long."

He was silent. The moment stretched on. In his expression stood compassion, affection and...flashes of desire.

She remembered herself and considered her hands. "There is something else I must have."

"Name it."

A knock came at the door.

"Come in," Killian ordered.

The butler appeared, tea tray in hand. He set the elements out on a table before them, then promptly turned on his heel and left.

"Would you do me the favor to pour?" Killian asked, motioning to the teapot and the service.

Relaxed in his presence, she agreed. Yet she knew she might not be so with her next request. She set about pouring tea, handing him his, offering the sandwiches and biscuits.

"Thank you," he said, took a sip of his tea and placed his cup aside. "I hope you didn't plan to return to London today?"

"No. I reserved a room at the inn in Ashford."

"Please don't go. Stay for dinner. Stay the night, in fact. The family's all here, waiting for Lily to deliver her baby. You know everyone from Marianne and Remy's wedding. No need to rush back to town today, is there? Not since we've agreed on your stipulations."

"That's kind of you but I don't wish to intrude on your family."

"You won't. Besides, you are family. No way out of this."

She narrowed her gaze on him, playful in her grin. "Are you getting your own way by manipulating me?"

He flinched. "Certainly not. I'm just citing logic. What do you say? Stay."

Oh, how she wanted to. Tired, exhausted by her anxiety and relieved at the outcome of this discussion with him, she could use a diversion. "I will."

"Wonderful." He picked up his cup and saucer.

"There is one more matter," she said, as she sat back and took a sip of her hot, comforting tea. To be quite emphatic about this issue, she should be forthright. And so she put down her cup, clasped her hands and said, "I will work for you for these houses. You buy my services as a decorator. The project is complicated, the houses many and it may require two years or more to complete."

He nodded once. "But?"

"Throughout it all, you and I will remain client and consultant. Home owner and decorator."

"Business associates?" he asked, his face placid.

Why, oh, why did her heart squeeze tight? "Correct."

"I agree."

You do? She forced a smile. "Thank you."

"My pleasure."

And why is it not also my own?

CHAPTER 8

"And I'm delighted, Olivia," said Pierce, hoisting a wine glass toward her, "that you've agreed to Father's proposal. I know he's pleased."

Liv grinned at Killian's son.

"And if Pierce is pleased," Killian said with a smile wreathing his face, "I know we all will do well."

"Pierce has become Papa's watch dog," Ada said as she raised her wine glass and lifted it in honor of her older brother.

"Wise to have two heads on a project," Lily offered gaily, her hands over her large pregnant belly. "Papa always needed a second he could trust. Pierce is that man," she turned to Liv next to her.

"He's done wonders for me," said Julian. "I would not have considered the threshers at the high price they were if not for Pierce's insights."

"Now, stop. I'm going to blush," Pierce said with a charming hint of pink to his cheeks. "It's what we're all about, isn't it? Making us all profitable."

The six sat at a circular table and the butler and footmen

had just come in with the brandy for the gentlemen. The ladies did not get up to retire.

Different from the usual custom of separation of the sexes after dinner, this family practice of remaining together pleased Liv immensely.

"We ought to make it the ordinary thing to ask you about everything we plan to buy, Pierce." Julian gazed at his brother-in-law with fondness.

"Provided he has the time," Ada said. "And that he's here and not in Paris or Berlin or Calcutta."

Pierce shook his head. "No, not Calcutta. I'm out of those negotiations. Decided I won't do the import-export business with Masters Company."

"Oh?" his father asked. "This is new. Why not?"

Pierce glanced down the table, his eyes dark. "You must not let this get out."

Julian said, "Oh, dear. You've gotten hold of a secret. I can tell. What's gone wrong with Bernard Master's shipping line?"

"I hear they're overextended. They've lost about five to six percent of their China trade to an American line."

"Ohhhh!" Lily cried. "Oh, oh, no!" She pushed back her chair and struggled to her feet, her horrified gaze on the floor.

Julian shot up, one hand round her back, another to her wrist. "What's wrong? Sweetheart?"

"I'm...I'm—"

Liv looked down at the carpet and knew at once Lily's problem. She rose and took the young woman's other arm. "You're fine, Lily. This is normal. Your waters have broken. Time to greet your baby."

Julian scooped his wife into his arms. "Get Perkins. We need to fetch the doctor in Ashford."

Killian strode to the doors to fling them wide for Julian.

"I'll get him," Pierce said and pulled the service bell in the corner.

"Come with me," Lily called over Julian's shoulder to Liv. Before dinner, they'd had a few minutes in the parlor to discuss birthing methods. The discussion cemented a friendship that had begun when they'd met at Marianne and Remy's wedding last October.

Liv smiled at Lily as she followed them to the hall. "Of course."

Julian, his handsome brow lined with concern, took the grand staircase with speed.

Liv ran to keep up. "I saw you picked at your dinner, Lily. Were you not hungry?" She had to know if she should expect Lily to have digestive problems during labor.

"I had those contractions you said were false. But they were strong. So I couldn't think of food, Liv."

"That's fine. Good, in fact. When did you last eat a full meal?" The young woman needed strength for the hours ahead.

"Luncheon."

"Good. Ah, you go, Julian. Get her comfortable. I need a few things. I'll be right up." She ran back down the stairs right up to Killian.

He stood, his face white, staring up at the stairs.

She put her hands to his chest and clutched the satin of his waistcoat. Beneath her fingers, his heart beat strong and fast. "Killian, she'll be fine. We'll make her comfortable and wait for the doctor."

"But if she delivers before he gets here—"

"She won't. Killian—" She put her fingertips to his cheek. His flesh was warm, his smoothly shaven jaw silk under her skin. "Look at me. She's safe and warm and in her own bed. She has her husband with her and all her family close to cheer her on."

His silver eyes flashed in pain. "But it's her first, Liv. You know all the things that can go wrong."

"Darling, listen to me. She's young and healthy. And you know these things take hours. Hours. We'll get the doctor here. And by tomorrow morning, you'll have your first grandchild. Think of that."

He caught her hand and squeezed hard. Then with gratitude in his gaze, he raised her fist and kissed it.

"Now where is that bottle of brandy?" she asked him with a grin. "Get it, Killian. Drink, will you? But first, show me the way to the kitchen."

❧

The sun split the dark of night from the horizon as Killian spun to the sound of Liv's footsteps. She walked toward Julian who sat, his head in his hands, in the hall chair. Ada had gone to bed hours ago. Pierce had stretched out on the settee in the parlor downstairs, his only companion a pot of coffee. Killian had stayed with Julian, pacing before the hall window countless times tonight.

Liv's sun-fire hair was down, her pins long since fallen or pulled out in her long vigil over Lily. Somewhere she'd found a ribbon and fashioned the wealth of it to stream down her back. The overall effect made her appear like a nymph from the sea. A tired nymph. For the duty she'd eagerly taken up to attend Lily in her first labor, she wore a huge white apron, loaned to her by the family cook. Her face seemed peaceful, her gaze steady with whatever she was about to impart.

Julian stared up at her. "News?"

"What?" Killian asked her, incapable of more.

"It won't be long now." She told Julian and said to Killian, "I can see the head of the baby."

"Oh, Liv," Julian groaned. "She sounds like she's splitting in two."

Liv went to her knees before him and squeezed his hands. "It's normal, Julian. She's doing well. You don't see her in between contractions but she's really strong and brave. Eager to see her baby, too."

"If only we had the doctor," he complained.

"I know. But we can't help that Elanna and Carbury summoned him first."

Killian could scarcely believe that Elanna had gone into labor with her child on the very night that Lily did. Pierce had taken a horse from the stables and ridden over to Carbury's house when the butler returned from town to say that the countess had requested the doctor hours before. When Pierce returned, he'd been white as sheets and Killian could only surmise he was afraid for Elanna, but also disturbed by Carbury. The two men had never gotten on. Carbury, wise in few things when it came to people, had long seen the attraction that Pierce had to Elanna. The earl was an irritable man, quick to anger, eager to judge, bent on ridicule. No wonder Elanna had become bitter, irrational.

"Listen to me, Julian," Liv beseeched him. "The baby comes. Soon. I don't know when but Lily's close to delivery."

"If he gets stuck. That happens to women. If she can't push him—"

"Julian, Julian. She's not frail. She's not petite. I know it's painful to sit out here and wait for news."

"Damn right. I'm going in." Eyes wild, he shot to his feet. "To hell with convention."

Off he marched and Liv staggered a step backward.

Killian caught her around the waist and let her rest against him. The feel of her in his arms was intoxicating. "Let him go. Might do them both good." He turned her around gently, lifted her chin and brushed tendrils of hair from her cheeks. "You're exhausted. But doing such a wonderful job."

She let her head hang back and she looked up at him through half-lidded, weary eyes. "Thank you, dear sir."

"Have you eaten?" The butler had ordered a full meal of beef and potatoes for everyone about three this morning. He'd delivered a heaping tray into Lily's chamber. The rest he placed in the dining room. None ate it. It cooled on the dining room table when Ada, Julian and Killian abandoned it to return back up the stairs to wait in the hall.

Liv closed her eyes and shook her head.

"I can have cook bring you anything you wish. Eggs. Bacon."

"Hot oats with cream." She inhaled deeply. "Coffee."

He could not resist. He drew her against his chest and buried his fingers up into the silken mass of hair at the crown of her head.

She sighed against him, her cheek to his chest like a long-lost friend. His first thought was that she trusted herself into his care. A shock. A delight. His second thought was how funny it was that his daughter was giving birth in a bed in that room beyond, and despite his own fatigue, all he could think of was getting this woman out of her clothes and into his own bed.

She burrowed against him. "I'll sleep for a week after this baby's born."

He dropped a kiss to her forehead. "Stay here and sleep."

She raised her face and smiled at him dreamily. "I may do just that."

And will you call me 'darling' again? "I hope you will."

The far door to Lily's suite fell open. "Liv! Liv! Come quickly!"

CHAPTER 9

"Oh, Killian," Liv whispered as she glided toward him minutes later with a bundle of blankets and baby in her arms. "Come greet your grandson."

Words abandoned him. This dark-haired writhing little cherub stared blankly up at him and waved his tiny little arms. Killian put out a finger to touch his eiderdown skin. *My God, thank you.*

"Lily did so well."

"No problems?" he asked recalling how Aileen had bled profusely after Ada's birth. They'd had a scare they might lose her, but once the doctor had delivered the placenta, she was well. That had not been so years later when Aileen and her next baby died in childbirth.

"None. She's laughing. Julian is beside himself."

"I'm sure. I remember."

"So do I. Such a joyous event, a new child in the family."

The baby fussed and she bounced up and down with him. "You can go in. She wants all of you to come in and tell her what a splendid job she did."

"Just like my girl to seek praise!" He chuckled, though his

throat was clogged with emotion. "I'll give the new parents time alone together. They'll have less of it from now on."

She laughed. "They will indeed. Lily says I'm to return just as soon as I introduce all of you to Garrett Quentin William Ash."

"How do you do, Garrett," Killian said with pride.

"I'll go find Pierce, if he's still awake." She made to leave.

"No, you won't. You'll sit in this chair. I'll get him. Ada too." He steered Liv to the wing chair he'd occupied all through the night.

She sank to it like a stone. "Thank you."

"And you need that breakfast."

"Not yet." She shook her head and smiled down at Garrett. "Lily wants to put him to the breast. We talked about it while she was in labor. She hates the idea that another woman would hold her child and share such intimacy with him. I don't blame her. The custom of a wet nurse is...well...cold."

"Whatever she wants, she should have. This is her child."

"I've done it and know its challenges. I promised I'd help her."

His heart swelled with gratitude to this woman whom he barely knew, save for his instincts that declared he must know her intricately. "That's so good of you. If her mother were alive, she'd be here to advise her. A servant wouldn't do. Thank you, Liv."

"You're welcome. I'm happy to do this for her. And you. Aside from all else, we are friends." She tipped her head and grinned. "I've called you Killian."

You've called me more than that.

Her gaze lingered in his and he wondered if she searched her memory for her endearment.

Garrett let out a long loud cry.

"Oh, my," she said, laughing. "Get Pierce, will you, please?

Ada, too, if you think she'll come quickly. This child is hungry and needs his mother."

◈

The clock in the hall downstairs in the foyer chimed noon before Liv emerged from Lily's bedchamber with Ashford's elderly doctor by her side. Killian, Pierce and Ada rose from their chairs to hear his prognosis.

"I'm happy to tell you, Misters Hanniford and Miss Hanniford, what I told His Grace. Her Grace is in excellent health. She is tired, as you might imagine, but she shows all signs of a quick and uncomplicated recovery. No need to worry on any count. The child is hale and hearty, feeds instinctively and can insist quite loudly when he wishes. You'll have a handful with that little fellow."

Killian thanked the man.

Ada sighed. "Wonderful."

But Pierce—his eyes weary, his black hair mussed and his clothes rumpled—jammed his fists in his trouser pockets. He'd had a hard night. On the day his mother died when he was just a lad of fourteen, he'd cried his heart out. "You're sure our Lily's well?"

This concern, Killian suspected, came from the comparable news the doctor had given them of the condition of Elanna, the Countess of Carbury, after the delivery of her own son. The countess had survived a very long labor of twenty-one hours. The baby had been breech and at first, had not breathed at all until the doctor cleared his mouth and nose. Whereas, Garrett had come without complications. Lily was eating well, had napped already and had nursed her baby boy twice to contentment on both their parts.

"I am, sir, confident that Her Grace will be up and about

in two or three weeks." The frail little doctor glanced at Killian and Liv.

Killian sensed the man did not wish to speak overly much about the horrendous scene he'd witnessed at the Carburys'.

Pierce frowned down at the doctor. "So Lily is not bleeding?"

"No, sir."

"Not hysterical?"

Killian winced.

Liv dropped her gaze to the floor.

The physician had told them of Elanna's and her baby's health immediately upon his arrival an hour ago. His statement—diplomatically worded as it had been—of Elanna's condition had given them all a start. The young mother, upon hearing that her son breathed, had sent him away to the nursery with the wet nurse she'd hired. She also refused to see her husband and had even banned him from her chambers.

"No, sir. Her Grace is chipper."

"Not like the countess?"

The doctor examined Pierce.

Killian saw the man was mystified by Pierce's continued interest in Elanna.

"Not like the countess, sir," the doctor said. "I did attempt to reassure His Grace as to his sister's condition. He told me he will ride over to visit her later this afternoon."

"But you said she told you she'd receive no one but the wet nurse," Pierce pressed him.

"That's true, sir. But I do believe that once she hears her brother wishes to greet her, she will relent."

"You don't know her," Pierce said between thin lips.

The doctor bristled. "Since she was a child, sir, I have known her ladyship to be charming and bright. She has, we all do know it, a few challenges at home. I have faith she will come round."

Killian had heard enough about the Carburys. Meanwhile, Pierce must get some sleep, clear his head and set his priorities on his sister. "Thank you for your attentions, Doctor. I'm sure my son-in-law has expressed his gratitude."

"He has, Mister Hanniford. My regret is that I was not available to you earlier, but with the challenges with the countess and her child, I feared the worst for both. Her Grace is in much better health and in all ways, too. However, you were very fortunate to have Lady Savage in attendance on her." The old man smiled at her ear-to-ear. "Nothing like a happy delivery, mother and child. Thank you, ma'am."

She inclined her head. "My joy to help."

"I will look in on Her Grace tomorrow. And now, if you will excuse me, please?"

"Of course." Killian stepped aside and the four of them watched him gingerly descend the stairs.

Ada said, "Well, my dears, this is my notice that I am going to take a long, long nap. See you at dinner."

Pierce took a look at Lily's bedchamber door. "I think I'll go for a ride."

Killian glared at him. "Be careful," was all he dared to say. *Don't go near Carbury Manor. Don't expect to be shown into Elanna's presence. Don't hope for anything from a married woman who's just given birth to a child she doesn't want by a husband she doesn't love.*

"I will. You needn't worry. I caught your concern, Father. I know when I'm about to make a fool of myself."

Only once had Pierce ever done an idiotic thing. He had forever regretted it and vowed never again to be so brash. This fascination with Elanna was becoming one he could not seem to end.

"And if you don't mind," Liv said with an air of relief, "I am off to the kitchen to eat a feast fit for the queen."

"Good idea," Killian said as he offered her his arm. "I've a need for part of that feast myself."

Killian and Liv sat in the servants hall at their long oak table to eat. As they dined on cold chicken, bread and lettuces from the kitchen garden, they imparted the most recent news of the doctor, mother and child to the cook and the two kitchen maids. A footman wandered in to listen, then the butler.

As each drifted away to their duties, Killian and she finished their meal.

Liv drained her tea cup. "Lily has asked me to remain for a week or two."

This put a grin on his face. "I hope you agreed."

"Do you mind?"

"Why in the world would I? Not an hour ago, we were friends. Your term." If she thought he'd hold her to that ridiculous stipulation that they remain client and consultant, he'd disabuse her of it. Maybe even kiss her to rid her of that idea. "You've helped my daughter give birth to the heir to the dukedom, my grandson, Ada's and Pierce's nephew. I'd say you are friend of the entire family. There are few walls between us."

She sat back in her chair and frowned. "Lily wants me to help her learn how to handle Garrett."

"There's no one better, I'd say."

"She's concerned. Doesn't know what to do. How to hold him. Why he cries."

"I know she'd be grateful." *I'd be delighted to have you here indefinitely.*

"There's a problem though. I have only my one valise. One gown. I need to go back to London and get a few clothes. I could catch the coach tomorrow and return the following afternoon."

"Tell me what you need. I'll get it for you."

"No, Killian. I cannot allow you to do that. It's not proper."

"You've been up all night and half the day. You're dead on your feet and want to travel to London by a coach constructed in the last century."

"Oh, come now! Not that bad."

"Almost!" He reached over and took her hand. "I won't let you go. Lily needs you. Garrett, too. How can you desert those who require your presence?"

She pressed her lips together.

"Stay and in the hours when you're not helping Lily, you'll be working with me."

"On the houses." She brightened, sitting taller at the suggestion. "Of course."

"You'll tell me what you like. Need."

"What I don't like too. We can take a drive to Ashford or Tunbridge. There are homes there that should be bombed."

She chuckled. "But the interiors? Ah, those have treasures centuries old. Tapestries and portraits and—"

"I'm an American, my dear." He'd almost called her his darling. She was, but he must wait to let her enjoy that. "I want what's new and exciting. I look forward not back."

She blinked at that and removed her hand from his. Whatever he'd said had sobered her.

Well, it was true. He looked to the future. Always. "The past is not a landscape I can change."

That sobered her. "I agree on that."

He wanted to take her hand once more but did not dare use more than logic. "Say you will stay and let me get what you need."

"Yes." She nodded and shook off whatever had obsessed her. "Perhaps if we sent one of the maids up to my house? I'd send a note for her to give my housekeeper with a list of items I'd like."

"I'll speak with Julian and I'm sure he'll agree." *I'll make my own list of gifts you'll have to fill your stay.*

"I don't mean to be a burden."

"Never. Now...is it time to go to rest?"

"Oh, it definitely is." She rose, took his arm and they made their way up to the ground floor and up the grand staircase. Midway, she missed a step.

He swept her up into his arms. Her surprise melted to surrender as he strode with her to the landing and down the hall to her door.

"Open it," he said and carried her inside. At the side of her bed, he set her down.

She turned in his arms, her hands cupping his neck. "Thank you."

What could he allow himself and still be a gentleman? Nothing but words. "You're welcome."

"You could let me go." She shook back her long red hair, her voice was half teasing, half warning him.

"Good business ethics," he joked.

She stroked the hair at his nape.

But he didn't release her and she didn't move. He grew hard, his blood racing with her touches.

"It's not fair to take advantage of a tired woman." Her eyes twinkled.

"I know." He grinned.

"You are a rogue."

"And you, Lady Savage, are a sweet temptation."

"I should insist."

"Hmmm. I suppose so." He considered the ceiling for a moment. "But this business behavior was all your idea."

"Woe unto me."

She gave him a saucy once-over and turned her back to him. "Do me the favor to unlace me?"

She'd brought no lady's maid. Lily had not assigned her

one. And given the nearness of her delectable body, he didn't wish to summon one. "At your service, my lady."

As she clamped two hands to the bedpost, his own hands shook. Desire rolled through him like thunder. He wanted her as he had not wanted any woman in more than a decade. He clenched his fingers and splayed them wide.

Turning, she caught his gaze. "Undo me," she said and turned back again toward the post to whisper, "You already have, you know."

"Minx," he murmured in protest and praise. He made nimble work of her buttons and pushed her gown from her delicate shoulders and down her graceful arms. Her back was lean, muscular. Her skin was flawless, pink, perfect. She was too ripe a temptation and he was too prudent to seduce the exhausted woman who has just helped his daughter bring her first child into the world.

"Step out of it," he ordered her and when she did, he picked up the gown to place upon the nearby chair. He untaped her petticoat and let it whoosh to the carpet. Then he set to untying her laces, listening to her tiny sighs of pleasure and controlling his desire to strip away the damn corset and replace it with his hands, his lips, his tongue.

He swallowed loudly.

She shrugged and the corset dropped down, down, down, over her petticoat, hooking on the cursed bustle and dropping to the floor. He untaped the bustle and her crinoline so that she stood only in her shift.

He itched to take that off, too. He breathed her in, her jasmine fragrance and hot little breaths of desire. With every inch of his rigid body, he willed her to be naked and natural in his arms. *But not now, man. Not now.*

He cleared his throat. "I'll leave you."

She didn't turn, didn't agree, but cupped her shoulders

and nodded. Then she whirled to face him, her dark brown eyes hungry. "You won't kiss me again?"

He pinched her nose. "You need your sleep. I need to go."

She looked forlorn, confused. "I do. But oh..."

"Liv, if I stay, we will go to that bed and enjoy ourselves."

She blinked, then laughed, coming back to her wits. "You'd get no joy of it. I can't lift a finger let alone make proper love to that blackguard Killian Hanniford."

She would welcome the passion that sparked between them. How could he be so fortunate? What had happened to her earlier denial of her interest in him? He'd have to ask, insist she tell him. *But not now.* He smiled at her, willing himself not to grab her and put her to the bed. "You're tired. I am too. We'll discuss this later."

She caught him by the ends of his cravat and it unraveled in her hand. "Oh dear, I cannot even detain you properly."

He chuckled. This ploy of hers was so sweet. But the time, the place was not right to claim all of her. "You could."

She tipped her head, a teasing smile upon her luscious lips. "How?"

"Call me darling again."

"Did I do that?" Her voice held uncertainty.

He said not a word, but arched one brow high.

She blushed, her cheeks pink. "I must've been dreaming."

"Do dream again."

And then she shocked him to his core.

She flowed against him, the suppleness of her breasts and belly the spontaneous invitation to passion he'd craved from her. Her hands flowed up his chest to frame his jaw, then to sink into his hair. Rising on her toes, against his lips she whispered, "I prefer the reality."

She skimmed her mouth along his, the brush of her flesh molten and angelic. She put the full of her lips to his and he was lost, gone to a bliss he'd forgotten existed, filled with the new rapture that was kissing Liv Bereston.

He set her from him.

She looked bereft, her mouth turned down.

He slanted two fingers across her swollen lips. "There will be more. Not here. Not now But soon."

She was so tired, she wavered.

He caught her up in his arms and seizing the will power that had forged him into a wealthy man, he set her to the bed. He yanked the coverlet over her. "Go to sleep. Rest."

She cupped his cheek.

Unable to deny her, he bent low, caught her hand and pressed it to his heart. With a tenderness he summoned from the fathomless well she'd shown him existed in her own soul, he kissed her magnificent mouth. "We need you. All of us."

CHAPTER 10

July 2, 1879

"I must go up to London," she told Killian as she closed her notebook and they ended their regular morning meeting about design and decor for his houses. "Roger will be eager to hear about our discussions. The town-house plans are as he drew them. And the major changes are to your own house."

"His original sketches were sound," Killian said. "He did a fine job. The biggest change we've made is to extend the foyer. I want that rotunda. Make it big, but not a wind tunnel. I've walked in the door of too many houses where the poor butler was nearly swept up to the rafters like a bird in the cross draft."

She grinned at him. "It shouldn't be difficult for Roger to redesign the foyer so that it sits forward of the main line of the house. With the *porte cochère*, a rotunda will look impressive but not opulent. Just as you want it. A home."

"Exactly. And be certain he understands that the most

important aspect is to turn left from the foyer, so anyone still has a view to the arches out to the sea."

"If only those arches could talk," she said with a thrill for how he saved them. "They'd shout their gratitude to you for preserving them."

Killian rose from behind the desk in the library. In his sky blue waistcoat and white shirt, he was the country gentleman at his leisure. London toffs might not approve of his appearance before her without his frock coat, but she did. Stripped nearer to his skin, she could admire his health and his natural male vigor. When younger, Killian Hanniford had surely been a heartbreaker. Now, he was devastating to any woman who saw him. And yet, she chastised herself for her desire for him, forbidden as it was.

Last night, he'd returned from his most recent visit to London. He and Pierce had gone to town five days ago to settle a negotiation that was going badly. Only Killian returned. When she saw him enter the salon last night, her heart had leapt in her throat.

That was so telling. While he'd been away, Liv had pined for him like a debutante for her first beau. One look at him and she'd lost her breath, pinning herself to her chair so as not to rush up to embrace him.

She'd been so good these past few weeks, not to touch him, not to kiss him. And he had not approached her intimately either. For that she was grateful. But angry too. At herself. At her past. Here was a man who elicited her every torrid feminine need and she should not countenance her infatuation. Nor should she encourage him to court her.

And yet...and yet she'd prized the other little tokens she could accept. The burn of his gaze on her own. The caress of his fingers as he took her arm and escorted her in to dinner or out to the gardens for a stroll in the moonlight. The scent of his cologne as he bent to turn the pages of the musical scores for her when she played the piano each afternoon in the small salon. As before, she didn't need the sheet music, but she did need his nearness, his attentions. God help her.

"Liv," he spoke to her as he stood before her chair. "Where are you? Dreaming again?"

Of you. Yes. She licked her lips, imagining she'd reach up and enfold him in her arms, absorb his magnetic strength, empowered with his might. But that was for naught. She'd told him months ago that they'd had their idyll on the shores of the Seine. But the true idyll had been here at Willowreach. In his presence. With his family. Near him, a step away, each day, each hour. Living with his ideas, his energy, his boldness. And his irresistible, novel optimism. One that was innate to his nature. As opposed to her own that was self-taught, deliberately nurtured.

And oh, she must pack. Must leave here. *Because I care so much. More than is allowed.*

"Liv." He reached out and for the first time since she'd kissed him the day Garrett was born, he touched her. Lifting her chin with two fingers, he smiled sadly at her. "I don't want you to go, Liv."

"I should," she said with a fearful determination borne of the longing for him that she'd experienced while he was away —and the painful memory of how she'd spent years damning him. "Lily and Garrett are getting on quite well. The new nurse they've hired understands her duties and they all have a suitable routine. They no longer need my advice."

His shoulders sagged. He dropped his hand. "I know she'll miss you."

"I've enjoyed every minute. All of you are so easy to be with." *Easy to love.*

"Then why not come to Paris with all of us for the christening of Marianne and Remy's son?"

The family had received a letter yesterday that Marianne

had delivered her baby three days ago. The young heir to the dukedom of Remy and the princedom of d'Aumale was to be christened Bertrand Andre Duquesne Marceau, after both of his grandfathers and his father. All the Hannifords planned to go to Paris to attend the ceremony the first of September and they had invited Liv along. Tempted to accept, she'd refused. Caution was best when the lure to remaining near Killian night and day could mean she'd succumb to her desire for him. Memories of how forward she'd been to call him darling and to kiss him made her hungry to taste his lips again. The memory did not shame her, as it might have years ago. She surprised herself. How long could one continue to condemn another? Negativity took such a toll on the body and mind.

But duty called, as did prudence. "I cannot, Killian. I have so much work to do. I must return to London to prepare my meetings for your furniture and upholstery, the rugs and ever so much more. Good furniture and draperies take so much time to construct. And we want to finish your house, especially, in a reasonable period of time."

She stopped, appalled she'd sounded like a nervous twit, rattling on about details.

"I won't rush the builder," he said. "Ten months is what he quoted me from the time he laid the foundation. I'm in no hurry. I simply want it done right. He predicts March at earliest, if we don't have much snow."

"Expect April," she told him, happy to change the subject. "Or early May."

He gazed down at her, his regard much too intimate to be comfortable. "When do you wish to go?"

"Tomorrow." *The sooner, the better.* Everything about him drew her like a magnet. In three weeks, he'd changed her view of him. Where was her loyalty to the sorrows of the past?

"Let me escort you back to town."

His concern ran through her like warm honey, lulling her with desire. She must object. "You've only just returned."

"I came as quickly as I could only to be with you again."

She turned her face aside and shut her eyes. "You should not make decisions like that based on an attraction that—"

"That we both feel?"

He went to one knee and took both her hands. "Look at me, please. Liv, you and I have developed an affection each other. You cannot deny it."

"I don't." *That's what eats at me.*

"I keep hoping you'll learn to trust me enough to tell me why you reject me."

"It's not a matter of trust, Killian." That was the truth. Could he understand her old hatred of him? He'd been her devil. The man who'd ruined her family.

"After that morning Garrett was born," he went on, "I hoped you were accepting our regard for each other."

She faced him, resolve to be brave strong in her mind but weak in her soul. "I did. You must see that on that morning when Garrett came in to the world, I was tired."

"You were spontaneous," he said with dancing eyes.

She stiffened. "You and I are not a good match in any way."

"I don't agree."

She tried to extricate her hands from him, but he would not let her go. "You must."

"Then you must tell me why."

She tore away and shot to her feet. *Why? Because society would howl if they learned I valued you. They'll surely denounce me when they learn I work for you. And then what will happen to my reputation? My clientele? My business and earnings? How can I support Camille?*

She whirled on him. "I owe you nothing."

The insult of her words made him blanch. "I do not agree."

Was that Killian Hanniford the hard-hearted negotiator?

She stared at him, a pain of realization stabbing her.

This man before her was not Hanniford, the terror, the thief, the robber. But Hanniford, the man who cared for her.

She had hurt him. She clutched her hands together. She hated her own actions. But how could she relent? "I return to London tomorrow. Then I'm on to Brighton to survey the properties. That is, if you still wish me to consult on design and interiors."

"I do." He stood before her, at once composed, the veneer of the consummate businessman, polite and congenial.

She'd wounded him. She saw it in the tick of a muscle in his jaw, the grey shadows in his eyes, the down turn of the corners of his mouth. *What have I done? I cannot bear to make him unhappy, but I cannot bear to remain and betray my parents' memories.*

"I want you to do this for me, Liv. Your expertise is what I need and want. For the months ahead as we work together, I promise you we will be as you wished. Strictly business associates."

The hole in the region of her heart opened into a pit. But she swallowed hard and said, "Thank you. I welcome the work. It's challenging and a project I'd like to complete. The land you've bought from young Lord Savage is a stunning bit of coast." *I long to see it again. Feel the wind in my hair. Absorb the sun on my skin. Hear the endless water crashing on the shore.* "And renovation of the townhouses is a unique challenge."

"By all means, then, continue to work on my house and the townhouses. I wouldn't deprive you of the chance to do great work because I overstepped your boundaries."

Like a gentleman, he was taking all the blame. She would not dicker with him. This catastrophe was hers, all hers. Her desire for him outpacing her own common sense. Well, no more. No more.

"Thank you. I appreciate your understanding," she said, but her heart was not in her words. Sadness was.

His hand out, he took a step toward her. "Liv—"

Had he seen her despair?

She could not deny how she cared for him. Even to work for him, she had to resolve her conflict about how she viewed him. He'd once been her nemesis. Now her employer. Her friend. To appreciate him more, she'd have to slay ghosts of her past. And those who might condemn her for associating with him now. Was she that strong? She stepped toward him—

"I say! My lord! Come back!" A man shouted in the hall. "My lord, you cannot go upstairs."

Killian whirled toward the door, a hand out to waylay her. "Stay here."

"Who is that?" she asked him as he jogged away and flung the door wide.

He stepped into the hall.

"Sir!" A man yelled. "Stop! You can't go up there!"

Liv recognized the voice of Perkins, the Seton family butler.

"Where is he?" shouted another man.

"My lord," Perkins bellowed, "His Grace is not here!"

A stocky man ran up to Killian and tried to go round him. "Out of my way, Hanniford."

Taller and more muscular, Killian grabbed his arm. "Carbury! Stop right there!"

Liv picked up her skirts and raced to the doorway. The earl whom she'd seen on a few occasions recently looked nothing like he had months ago at his wedding. He'd gained weight, a considerable amount. His round face was red, apoplectic. And his anger was a rage.

"Let me go, you cur!" he blustered at Killian.

Killian had him by his lapels. "What's the meaning of charging in here like a mad bull?"

"To hell with you, Hanniford. Where's Julian?"

"Sir?" the butler, panting, had caught up to Carbury and Killian.

"I have him, Perkins," Killian assured the servant.

"Where's Julian?" Carbury demanded.

"His Grace," Killian took care to enunciate his son-in-law's title, "is out consulting with his tenants."

"I need to see him."

"I doubt you will be granted an audience with His Grace when you barge into his house like a lunatic."

Carbury, up on his toes because Killian held him at attention, sneered at his captor. "Oh, I'll see him to be sure. His idiot sister is a whore. He'll see me or I'll throw her out. How will he like that, eh?"

"You're crazed."

"I am. No doubt with cause, Hanniford. Get me Julian. Get him now."

"I'll go," the butler said. "I'll send a footman down to the cottages."

"You do that," Carbury said, his wicked little eyes on Killian.

"Where can we put this man?" Killian asked the butler while his gaze remained on Carbury.

The earl scoffed. "You will address me as I should be. I am, to you, 'my lord'."

Killian scoffed. "You are, to me, nothing."

"The small parlor, Mister Hanniford," said Perkins. "We'll put him downstairs in the back parlor."

"Very well. Do come along, Carbury." Killian pulled him from the wall and walked him toward the stairs.

Liv watched them go, her heart beating frantically.

"What's wrong?" Lily appeared, Garrett in her arms, at the door to her chambers. "Who's yelling?"

Liv strode to her. "The earl of Carbury is here demanding to see Julian."

Lily approached the railing and leaned over to watch Carbury and Killian descend the staircase. "Trouble with Elanna?"

"It seems so. Yes." Liv curled an arm around Lily's waist. "Come back to your rooms."

"She should never have married him," Lily said. "She's hated him almost from the moment they were engaged."

Liv could utter compassionate words to her, but thought such sentiments less than useful. "Let Killian and Julian handle it."

"I worry about their son."

Of course she did.

"Elanna has no idea how to care for a small baby. I didn't. And she's without her mother as I was. Nate will suffer, poor mite. Fortunate me, that I have you as a friend."

"And I with you as my friend, Lily." She steered her back into her chamber and indicated she should sit in one of her Chippendale chairs.

"I fear what she'll do," Lily said, her eyes on the hollow of the fireplace.

Liv took one of her hands. "Please don't worry. You'll convey that to young Garrett and he won't understand why. Let your father and your husband handle Carbury."

"I'm telling you, she is a slut!" Carbury yelled.

At the violent words rising up from the hall, Lily's eyes went wide. "Dear god. What is wrong with that man?"

A door slammed shut.

Other male voices rose up the staircase.

Lily jumped to her feet and raced to the hall, the baby in her arms.

Liv was right behind her.

They stood, horrified at the scene below them.

In the beauty of the pink marble foyer, three angry men faced one another.

"You came quickly, Seton!" Carbury taunted Julian. "Wise of you. Tell this man to release me."

"I'd say he must have reason. I saw your carriage from the cottages. Saw my footman running toward me. What do you want, man?" Julian strode to his brother-in-law.

"Heed my words, Seton. Your sister goes too far. Restrain her. Put a bit between her teeth."

"What's happened?"

"She insults me. Shames me. I'll not have it. You're to blame. Stop her or—or else!"

"Do not threaten me, Carbury!"

The earl lunged for Julian.

"Oh!" Lily gasped.

"Let me go!" Carbury demanded of Killian who still had him by the arm.

Julian advanced on the earl. "You go home and make amends to my sister. I have no idea what you've done to her but she's become another person since she married you. Before, in fact."

"She's become a witch," the man spat back.

"You have yourself to blame."

"Her blame. All of it. Her blame and that solicitor of yours that you've sent to her."

Liv had no idea who that was.

Carbury gloated. "She fancies him. Smiles and coos, sends for tea and whisky. And him? He looks at her with his huge frog's eyes. Did you know he came yesterday? Yes, he did. For his monthly meeting, he called it. She locks the door behind them when he comes, always has. Why, eh? Why?"

"Phillip Leland sees her at my order," Julian said. "I told

you that. I will not change it. Let him in or I shall have the sheriff to enforce it."

Carbury fumed. "He is her lover."

"He is her friend," Julian said with solemnity.

Carbury laughed loud and long. "Friend? No, never. Makes me wonder if this baby is truly *my heir*?"

Julian went quite still.

"Is he?" Carbury tried to step closer to Julian, but Killian held him in place. "We'll see, won't we? If he keeps that watery blond hair or those droopy blue eyes."

Julian was slow to speak. "The most lamentable characteristic of my sister's personality has occurred since she pledged herself to you, Carbury. Whatever has befallen her is for you to remedy. I suggest you do it for both your sakes as well as that of your son." Julian turned to one side, his arm out toward the front door. "Now you may leave."

"I do not want that man in my house again. You tell him that, do you hear me?"

Julian advanced on him and met him nose-to-nose. "Never."

"If he darkens my door, I will kill him."

Julian did not seem to breathe. "I will warn him to go armed."

Carbury recoiled, then resumed his bravado. "Do that. A pistol will do him no good. He'll die anyway because if I don't shoot him, she'll eat him alive."

"Leave."

The earl pulled at the points of his waistcoat and then the tails of his coat. "I've warned you."

"Now, Carbury! Or I throw you out," Julian said.

Julian and Killian moved not a hair as Carbury stalked around them and slammed shut the front door.

"Marvelous weather today." Liv attempted to lighten the mood of both men in the carriage. "I would bet the sun is wonderful in Brighton today."

Killian attempted to smile at her. "Windy, too."

Julian and Killian sat opposite her as the Seton traveling coach crossed the Thames to enter London. They'd all set out together after breakfast this morning and for the past few hours, the men had been silent, lost in thought, brooding.

"I hope you'll be able to enjoy yourself while you're there the next few weeks," Killian said.

She'd told him she planned to stay three weeks in the coastal town to acquaint herself with the painters and drapers with whom she'd not worked in a few years. "I'm sure I will."

"Do come stay with me in Piccadilly, Julian," Killian said to his son-in-law. "No use to disturb your small house staff for only one night. Mine is still in residence and up to task. Besides, I wish to hear how your discussion goes this afternoon with Phillip Leland."

"He'll be undeterred by Carbury's bluster," Julian said with assurance. "Aside from the fact that he carries out my orders to call upon Elanna each month, he welcomes the chance to see her."

Killian's dark eyes widened with understanding. "He cares for her?"

"God help him, he does. Always has. I blame myself for this crisis. After she was indifferent to Lily and me when my father died, I wanted someone to be in contact with her regularly. I wanted her to know that someone cared about her. She wouldn't see me or Lily. But I always worried about her after she married Carbury. Now I worry Carbury may take revenge on Phillip."

"If he loves her as you say he does, he may not take heed to your warning," Killian said.

"Yes. I know. He's always been hopelessly in love with her.

I should not have presumed upon him to do this work. I should have known that if Phillip saw her often, he'd hurt himself as well as incite Carbury's jealousy. The two of them love her too much."

Killian winced and turned away from Julian to glance out the window.

Was he reflecting on how his son Pierce also found Elanna fascinating? Liv had witnessed how devoted Pierce was to that young woman. And yet she saw no characteristics in that lady which merited such enchantment. Indeed, the countess seemed spoiled, self-centered, irrational to the point of compulsion. Nor did she seem interested in changing.

"I don't know how she manages it," Julian said, shaking his head and crossing his arms.

"What's that?" Killian asked.

"She draws men to her. Many men. I can't say she lures them on purpose. She'd not ruthless. Yet she's never found any one man she favors. And that was part of her problem in the two Seasons she was out. She said she never met a man she cared for enough to marry. Then we had no means for her to carry on another Season and she married Carbury. Bad enough we have her acting like a Bedlamite, now we have Carbury too."

Rejecting her newborn child was not the action of a rational person. Instinct alone would drive a mother to hold her baby, cuddle him, nurse him and coo to him. But according to all who told tales of life at Carbury Manor—a dairy maid who came to deliver cream to Willowreach, the doctor, and the earl himself—Elanna had not relented. She ignored her child. The same way she ignored her husband. And by that act, tormented him.

Liv understood that behavior all too well. "Does she know anyone who did the same?"

The two men turned to her with surprise on their faces.

She felt the heat rise to her cheeks. "Forgive me. I should not have asked."

Julian stared at her. "Don't apologize. Yes, of course, she has a model for her actions."

A dark moment of silence passed in the coach.

But Julian sighed and looked from one to the other. "My parents. Our parents. Yes, did exactly that. Not quite in the same way. Both took delight in torturing the other with affairs or rumors of them. I don't recall my mother totally abandoning my care or Elanna's. But she might as well have done. She might be the model upon which Elanna takes her cues."

"So many take out their failures on others who should bear no suffering," she said. "I know. We had a member of our family who did that." *My father. Poor man.* "Hated himself and ridiculed all in his path for their foibles and faults. Bedeviled."

"I cannot allow Phillip to suffer," Julian said on the thread of sound. "Or be hurt by Carbury. Elanna must take responsibility for her own actions. Become responsible. Sensible."

She may not be able to do that.

Liv pushed the hideous thought away. Leaning forward to catch a glimpse of the shops and parks, she noted that they passed the Bank of England in the financial district. The Seton family solicitor, Phillip Leland, would have his offices nearby.

The coach idled. The footman pulled open the door and Julian alighted.

"After your meeting, will you come stay in Piccadilly, Julian?" Killian asked. "Please do."

"Thank you. I think I will. I'll need good company when I'm done here."

They said their farewells and the coach resumed its way winding west across town.

Killian's gaze was warm and probing. "Who was it that was so outlandish in your family?"

She shifted and wished she'd not opened this topic. "My father. Later, my mother, too. A pity for them, since they had a good marriage, and we were a sound and happy family..."

"Until?"

She took in his sympathy. But she could not answer.

He moved to her side of the coach and took her hand. "Happy until what?"

"Catastrophe struck. And he could not recover."

"I'm sorry," he said with compassion and the apology was not lost on her for the irony of it. And its solicitude.

She caught back hot tears.

He raised her hand, turned it over and dropped a kiss into her palm. Through the fabric of her glove, she recognized his earnestness. That too made her throat thick with unspent tears.

"Don't cry, Liv. Come to dinner tonight with us. We will be three morose gentlemen in need of good company."

"I cannot." She inhaled and shook her head. *No, enough of this delight in Killian Hanniford. Enough of his family and their unbounded support of each other. Their joy in each other and their dogged understanding of failure and despair.*

"I want to insist. Business associates do, you realize."

She slid her hand away. "Thank you. But no. I have much to do to move to Brighton. I have my lists of items I must find in Paris shops and I need to write to my vendors and plan my visit there. Then I must go south and find a small house to rent while we finish your houses."

"Then you need a good dinner."

"Killian, no. We are client and consultant. Friends at most."

His silver eyes dimmed. He did not reach for her hand again.

And when the coach came to a stop before her townhouse door, Killian alighted first.

"I do not expect to come south for another two weeks or more," he said as he took her hand to help her take the step to the street.

"That gives me a good start. By then, the builders may have begun erecting the frame for your cliff house. Perhaps even have spruced up the foundations of the townhouse block. I'll have much prepared for you to review."

"Do that. Thank you."

"If you decide to go to Paris, please write to tell me the dates you're there," he said.

To walk the boulevards with him would be bliss.

"We'll go to the *Sèvres* factory together."

She chuckled at the absurdity of Killian Hanniford choosing dinner service. "You want new china, do you?"

The smoldering look on his face said he wanted her. Only her.

She could not breathe.

"I want everything, Liv."

She wanted his beautiful mouth. His hands on her. His affections.

"I want china and fine tapestries. Good Lyon silk and your opinions on new art for the main salon. I want to drink with you, dine with you, dance. All of it."

To drink champagne with him at the Ritz and buy paintings from the new impressionists up in Montmartre lured her like a fly to honey. "You'd want a piece of sculpture, perhaps?"

He nodded, his eyes twinkling in delight. "By Remy? Yes, if any is appropriate for a home. I'd also like at least one painting by that new female artist who's becoming popular."

She grinned, happy for the lighter subject. "Marianne Duquesne?" Marianne Roland had not taken her famous husband's family name professionally, but used her maiden name. She said she would not trade on Remy's fame, but wished to earn her laurels on her own merit.

"Would you assist me with buying art in Paris, Liv?"

I shouldn't. "If the timing seems right."

Fires burned in his brilliant eyes. "It would be strictly business."

"Strictly business."

CHAPTER 11

Liv climbed the hill, her small leather reticule in one hand, her hat in the other. The sun streamed down, so bright and warm that she was happy she'd donned her lightest cotton gown on this hot July Saturday afternoon. The stone masons and carpenters would be at home on their half day of rest, enjoying their suppers with their families. The terrain to the top was clear of brush, thanks to the crew that labored to level the drive and the gardens for Killian's country home. She had easy walking up the steep terrain. For days, she'd yearned to come here this afternoon and be alone with the sun and the sea. Could the heat bake her mind and the wind free her body of her never-ending debate about how much she missed Killian Hanniford?

She picked her way up the hillside to the cliff and muttered to herself about her conflict. She couldn't rid herself of it. Her need to see Killian. Her fear that next week she'd meet with him and want his kisses so badly that she'd act like a hoyden. Occupying herself well each day, she worked hard and bent to her work, her choices of Bath stone for the corner quoins in the townhouses, the baked roof tiles, the plumbing pipes for the cisterns and the roasting oven ironwork. And more, so much more. She was grateful for the wealth of it, the details she had to master. But at dusk when she returned to her neat little house facing the sea, he invaded her thoughts. She'd dismiss her maid, her only servant here at the seaside house. She often cooked her own dinner and then she would sit at her bay window, her view out to sea. And he would come to her.

He stood before her, alluring as the devil, grinning at her, putting his hands on her, eliciting a contented sigh. And she'd blink. Become aware and chase him away. Yet he'd return to the edges of her consciousness, lingering, teasing her with what might be. And what was not.

What did he do tonight? Where did he dine? Who enjoyed his company? What lady of London claimed his attentions? His smiles?

"I'm quite mad with it," she murmured as she lifted her skirts high to side-step the bigger rocks. Thank heavens, her two heavier petticoats lay abandoned on her bed in the little townhouse she'd let on the Marine Parade. With them on as well as her ridiculous corset and bustle, she would have become a puddle in this heat. Today, she craved freedom.

Fortunately she'd grabbed her straw hat with the widest brim and run out the front door to go up into the public carriage she ordered for herself today. The hackney driver had become her friend, arriving for her each weekday morning at nine. He'd arrived for her this noontime, fetching her for this special trip. He asked why she came again this afternoon. She'd told him she needed the solitude. Work on the townhouses proceeded apace, the pesky problems with the wooden staircases solved. Work on Killian's country house was on schedule, the foundation completed, the wood frame half up, the plan to join the new house to the terrace measured and plotted.

What she did not tell her coachman was her true purpose here today. Her one desire was to stand and face the sea, enjoy the wind in her hair and inhale the fragrances of the abundant wild flowers growing on the leeward side of the medieval arches. Jealously, she'd wanted time to enjoy the view alone without interruption by workmen.

As she cleared the top of the ridge, she stopped and put down her reticule. Always the view through those arches made her heart skip a beat. She pressed her palm to her chest. The sight had soothed her when she'd been a child. The blue sea through the faded ivory stone curved like repeated frames over a panorama. Killian would get to see this view each day. Morning, as the sun dawned on the crests of waters floating west from the Normandy coast of France. Afternoon, as the rays burned into the sea and turned it green or gold or grey with rain. Evening, as the moon rose to waltz on the waves as the sea met the sky in a velvet blanket of night and stars twinkled in the void.

A gust of wind lifted her hat and she reached out a hand to snatch it back.

"I've caught it. Not to worry."

She turned to the sound of Killian's assurances and she beamed at him. Loneliness fled, her sad companion since the day she'd last seen him. *Good riddance.*

He strode the few steps toward her, a smile wreathing his handsome face, her hat in one hand, his own straw bowler in the other. He wore tailored buff trousers, a red waistcoat and navy frockcoat. To all who would see him, he appeared the prosperous gentleman, attired for his day of leisure in the sea-side town of Brighton.

"You surprised me! Thank you." She put a hand to her brow to admire every inch of him in the sunlight. He handed over her hat and she put it down on the stone ledge. "I didn't know you were coming. I thought your note said next week?"

"It did." He examined her, leaving nothing out of his perusal and making her feel self-conscious and oh, so desired. "I decided to come early. I needed a report. My designer, you see, writes infuriatingly short letters."

"You should have told her," she said, wanting to tease him and kiss him and... No. No she didn't. "She'd be more detailed."

"I took it as a good excuse to come," he said as he walked around her right up to the opening between two of the arches. He stood a moment, hands on his hips, inhaling the salt air deeply. "My lord. I'd forgotten this."

She moved next to him. "Remarkable, isn't it?"

He only shook his head and leaned over, two hands upon the stones and surveyed one end of the beach to the other. "On a clear day, you can see for miles."

She pointed, her arm out toward the east. "In the morning, you can almost detect the roof of Osborne."

"Queen Victoria's summer house?" he asked, smiling and pleased.

"Yes." She liked him happy and tickled, marveling at the world. Like this, he was not any of those hideous names many called him. He wasn't Black-hearted Hanniford or Hanniford, the Bastard, or the rebel blockade runner.

"And west? What's to see there?"

"The shore. The cliffs."

"So white."

"Yes. Chalk. Limestone."

"But the pebbles on the beach are brown," he said. "Why?"

"I've heard our masons say they're flint, hard polished sand. If you're available tomorrow, we can ask them to describe how they came to be."

He seemed content with that, his eyes still on the coast.

"Your family owned this land." It wasn't a question, but definitely an inquiry.

"My husband's family did, yes. I'm not certain the year. Although my father-in-law told me that his grandfather had purchased the land at the turn of the century when the Prince Regent was building the Pavilion. Then anyone who was society came to curry his favor, eat at his dining room table and gaze up at his enormous dragon hanging from the ceiling."

"The Prince had a dragon in his dining room?"

"He did. Made of silver. Hanging from the dome to hold a thirty-foot-long chandelier. A Chinese dragon for good luck."

"Anything money can buy, eh?"

"When some starve, it's heinous to buy frivolous things," she said on a sigh.

"I agree."

Over the years, after the catastrophe with her father and mother, she'd always ask acquaintances for details about him and his businesses. She'd learned much about the small Irish boy who'd immigrated to America with his older sister. How he'd worked the docks, learned to sail, bought a frigate for a song, then won another gambling. How as a ship owner, he'd once saved Negroes on a sinking slave ship off the coast of Florida. Set them free in Baltimore. She'd heard how he'd built a factory in Baltimore of stone and ordered windows installed for fresh air to flow in. "Is it true that you pay your factory workers well?"

"I pay them better than many a man. Yes." He frowned and faced her one hip to the stones, his arms crossed. "Do you think my house here is frivolous?"

"Let's see," she teased him. "With electricity, bathrooms with running water, efficient w.c.s and four lifts?"

He winced. "Tell me."

"Not frivolous. You've created it as a retreat. A home for entertaining. A seaside escape."

"With ten bathrooms with running water? Electric wires for lights? Four lifts? How is that different from other rich men's new country homes?" He cocked a dark brow.

"It's not pretentious."

Now he raised both brows. "You're certain?"

"If it were, you'd have two drawing rooms, a smoking room, a library as well as an office. And you've no ballroom, either."

"And the four lifts?"

She laughed. "Two to carry hot food to the table? One to carry luggage up to the second floor? The other for furniture?"

"Yes, those."

"Well, as I read the house plans, sir, none of those are for you. But for the health and welfare of your servants."

He pursed his lips and glanced back at the sea. "The house is not a folly?"

"It is large. Huge," she said with conviction. "But the abundance of bedroom suites with plumbing declares that the house is for your family. Your ever-growing family."

Slowly, he nodded, seeming content with her answer.

She smiled at him and swept out a hand. "But the element that ensures the house will be a haven for all Hannifords is this."

"You like it?" he asked, proud but seeking her approval.

She let her expression tell him the answer. "You are so wise to preserve it, Killian. Generations will thank you."

"Will you like it?"

"Oh, yes," she said with passion borne of her weeks working on it and having been given a free hand on so much. "The stone masons have shored up the base all around.

They've cleaned the stones, repaired the cracks. It is spectacular."

"I want you to love it."

That sucked the air right out of her lungs.

He narrowed his gaze on her mouth. He parted his lips, said her name, but then he turned away.

Her hope that he'd kiss her died.

He ran a hand through his ruffled hair. "Do you have any ideas why your husband's grandfather bought this land? It's not inside Brighton proper, but nearer Hove. Brighton would have been the more fashionable site, more expensive."

She shrugged, disappointment rife in her veins. "One buys what one can afford. I think they owned a house in town, too. To keep up with society. The family hoped to build here, but never did."

"Yet you know this land. How is that?"

"My husband's family liked to pack hampers and come up here to picnic. My parents were distantly related and we lived near them in London. We were invited to come along to Brighton for a week or more. All the children clamored to come because we thought we'd find gold."

He grinned at her, his black hair glistening like ink in the sun. "I've heard this story. Templars' buried treasure, isn't it?"

"A few escaped France after King Phillip destroyed the order in the early fourteenth century. They came here and hid for many months in the abbey. The Dominicans welcomed them, or so legend says, even though there wa no love between them."

"Why not?"

She took a seat on the stones of one arch. Through her thin shift, drawers and gown, they warmed her and she welcomed it. "Some thought the Templars hid the Holy Grail and refused to give it up. Other orders condemned them for it."

He turned around to gaze at the verdant green downs stretching north. "And has anyone ever found any gold coins here?"

"Not that I know."

"Good." He came away from the wall, his gaze delving into hers. "It's all mine now and I'm glad of it. What I find here is beyond price."

A frisson of joy rippled through her at what sounded like a compliment to her. Did she dare to reciprocate? "I find it beyond measure myself."

"Wonderful. Come with me down to the town. We'll have luncheon at the hotel and you'll tell me what you've been doing for these past two weeks."

She hung back. Her old fear that being seen on his arm in public would spark gossip she could not fight. *The Brighton Gazette* published columns called 'Arrivals and Departures'. Each week in black and white, names appeared not only of those who came to town, but also where they stayed and if they'd rented a house for the season or rooms in the local hotels. When they went home, their names appeared again including the date they left and what their destination was. If the paper also printed where these people went and with whom, Liv hadn't noticed. She'd been too horrified to read further.

"What's wrong?"

"Nothing. I—" To hell with fear. She was with him here. Just as she'd wished. Could she not have a few minutes fun? That had been so rare in her life. "A moment's thought that I might not be attired for the dining room."

"Nonsense. To me you are lovely in anything." He offered his arm.

She looped her own through his, smiling like a girl being courted.

He took a step, then stopped and patted her hand. Turning, he leaned back and scooped up her hat from the stones. Her reticule, too, he picked up. Grinning he handed them over. "The sun can blind you."

That and the power of your smile.

Taking his arm, she strolled into the pale pink stucco tea room of the Royal Albion Hotel and one sweep of the room told her that she knew none of the twenty or more other patrons.

She could ignore them. And enjoy her escort.

What a presence he made.

Killian commanded the room. His elegant tailoring declared him a man of means. His height and his bold dark looks combined to make him a superb specimen of masculinity. He requested the far corner table, secluded by potted palms and one large statue of an artfully clothed Aphrodite. He ordered the finest champagne from the menu, the best *hors d'œuvre* from the tray. He asked her for her preference for soup and *entrée*, then ordered the next six courses himself.

"I will waddle out of here," she told him on a laugh when the waiter departed.

"You need a full meal."

She shot him a rueful look. "I've never been accused of being undernourished."

He blinked, his bright eyes twinkling, his own expression feigned laughter, as if...as if he fought with himself not to assess her form. "We have a full afternoon and evening. Appointments. One after another."

"With whom?" she chuckled, delighted, alarmed. "It's Saturday."

"A porpoise."

"I'm sorry..."

He gave a laugh. "You have not been—I take it—to the Brighton Aquarium?"

She shook her head. She passed the Brighton Aquarium each day on her way to and from the sites. Developed as amusement for those who came to Brighton to take the sea-bathing cures and simply to enjoy the air, the aquarium showed sea turtles, giant prawns and multitudes of fish of the Atlantic. At night, concerts were given on the promenade. Singers from so-called London 'opera houses' sang popular ditties. Bands played. People chimed in and enjoyed themselves. "I haven't the time."

"Today, you do. Today, you will." He sat silent as the waiter popped the cork on the champagne. "We'll see this porpoise a local fisherman caught and donated. And as we walk I want to hear you tell me about the local draper you've chosen."

"The draper. Hmmm." Surely, he was toying with her. "But I'm most certain I had written you about him."

"Tell me again. I forget."

"That, I sincerely doubt," she said with a toss of her head.

He picked up his goblet. "To my decorator."

She raised her crystal and tipped it toward him. "To my employer."

"So tell me about the draper." After a healthy drink, he put his glass down and locked his gaze on hers.

She took another sip and licked her lips, amused by the challenge. "His family has been in business here since before Prinny ordered curtains from his father to hang in his bathroom in the Pavilion."

"Prinny's bathroom. I see. The man had one?"

"He did. Needed it for his gout. A walk-in tub."

"Ah-hah. Wonderful. So the draper's ancestry shows him to be qualified to handle silk from Lyon and Nanking?"

"It does."

"Sound credentials." He took a sip, then waggled a finger at her champagne. "Keep up with me. The waiter won't come unless both our glasses need refilling."

"You're quite sure I like champagne?"

He faced her squarely. "I am."

"How?"

He smiled as he drank. "I know a lot about you."

She froze. "You've asked about me?"

"No. I'm observant, Lady Savage. I've watched you at weddings and dinners and everywhere in my daughter's house. For three weeks, to be precise. You love champagne. Drink up."

She'd been so lonely without his company and she was so charmed by his appearance to sweep her away to buy her luncheon that she couldn't argue with him. Or refuse him. "I could get drunk."

"Since you rarely have more than two glasses, my answer is that you don't."

"I must watch you more closely."

His face fell. His gaze caressed her own. "Please do."

Like his invitation to her to kiss him again, this flustered her. She'd never had a beau who attempted to seduce her and so the thrill of Killian's attention left her as bubbly as the champagne. She searched for witty words. And couldn't find any. "What else have you observed?"

"That up on the cliff you were so happy to come with me, you nearly forgot your hat and your reticule. And now, you've not noticed that I hold your hand."

She sat bolt upright and slid her hand from under his.

"No one noticed. You're safe, Liv," he assured her.

She hadn't been safe since the first day she laid eyes on him. "Shall we visit the porpoise?"

He studied her, inhaled, then glanced away, searching for and hailing the waiter. "Of course."

CHAPTER 12

The horses clomped their way along the cobbles along the Marine Parade. Killian had given the cabbie her address. The driver, curse him, chose a quick route. Even the crowds conspired because everyone in Brighton seemed to have deserted the streets and returned home as the sun sank in the sky.

Killian hated to let Liv go. Their day had been perfect. She had been perfect. A companion who laughed and joked. One who forgot to look around her at every corner to see whom she might know. But he could not dismiss the questions her previous actions raised. They nagged at him. Was she afraid of who might see him? Or them together? Or who would disapprove of him?

He could think no other.

Yet, during the afternoon, she'd been on pins and needles less and less until in the pub minutes ago, she had forgotten her qualms.

At the aquarium, in front of the sea lion exhibit, she'd taken her usual cursory assessment of the crowd and discovered no one who put her on guard. Afterward, he'd led her along the walkway on the beach. No one there made her wary, either, thank god. He bought them lemon ices from a stall and, like children, they propped themselves up against a large boulder as they ate and watched the world walk by. The winds caught her glorious hair, lifting long enticing red tendrils of it from her pins and transforming her into a younger woman who laughed up at the sun and on a jolly Saturday outing, sparred with her suitor.

If she didn't yet consider him a suitor, he told himself to be patient. Today had been the launch of his plan to learn if she cared for him. He'd been lonely in London, missing her spontaneous laugh, her quick wit and those devastating moments when she sat simply caressing him with her dark enticing gaze.

He grinned to himself and forced himself to look out the window. She definitely did care for him. He noted how often and how carefully—and maddeningly—she had to pull back her hand when she reached out to touch him. Restraining herself at the last moment of realization made her eyes widen, her long red brows arch. Surprising herself, she could not stop herself from drowning in his fond regard for her. Watching him, she'd let her mouth fall open with desire, and catching herself, she'd lick her lips in need of his own. *So much for today*.

Tomorrow, he'd walk with her to church, if she wished to go. He'd buy her lunch again and find some other activity to keep her by his side. He'd make a picnic for the cliff, just like she'd done as a child with her husband's family. Monday, they'd go to the draper. He'd want to talk with the stone masons. And what would he do with her Tuesday? Take her dancing. If they had dance halls open on Tuesday nights, would she allow his arms around her? Would she waltz? Would she remain in his arms, her luscious body, firm and strong, lining his, luring his? He grew hot, filled with the urge to press her near. But if he crossed the carriage to sit beside her, she'd withdraw.

Tomorrow, man. Tomorrow. Or the next day, he'd kiss her, embrace her, show her that she fit him physically, emotionally. And after that, he'd ask once more if she'd come to Paris. For business. For pleasure.

"Come spend the week with me," he'd offer. *Let me pamper you and please you as you deserve to be.* She'd stay at the Grand Hotel near the Opera Garnier. Not with him in his house in Boulevard Haussmann. That was not appropriate. Not for what he ultimately wished for them.

Which was...marriage?

Marrying anyone had not entered his mind. Not in all these years since Aileen died. Why now? Why this woman who had eluded him? Why this woman who gave him conflicting signs that she cared for him, but didn't care enough to wish him close?

She challenged him. Thwarted him. Few women ever did. For her strength, he valued her. For her tenacity to build a profession, he admired her. For her generosity to his family, he praised her.

But did he love her?

He might. He might.

"Thank you for today, Killian," she said, intruding on his reverie. "I've never drunk so much beer."

He'd taken her to a pub where women were welcome and the beef and mash went down all too easily with beer from the keg. "That pub has been in business since your King Charles."

"How do you know?"

"When I was here, first looking at properties, I toured the town. This pub I like a lot. They know a bit about feeding the masses. Even inviting women inside the back parlor."

"I'll have to let out my corset tomorrow."

Or leave it off entirely. Lest his lecherous thoughts show on his face, he nodded at the street. "Almost home."

She cast her eyes to the floor of the cab.

"Would you like to go to church with me tomorrow morning?"

She got that haunted look in her eyes. "No. Thank you."

"Well, then afterward. I shall call for you. Noon." He couldn't allow her to dismiss him one more time. "We'll go to dine at the Albion."

"No. You'll come to my house for dinner."

The surprise of her intimate offer overjoyed him. "You cook?"

She cocked a brow at him. "I do. Quite well, actually. What do you like?"

"Roast beef. Potatoes, carrots. Anything. Everything." *You.*

"All of that?" She was chuckling.

"When did you learn how to cook? Did you do it when you were married?"

"Oh, no. Ladies do not cook. Or I didn't. David would not have allowed it."

"He restricted you? From cooking?"

"Ah," she said and raised a finger in the air. "A viscountess does not cook. She has staff. A cook and a scullery maid. A kitchen big as a stable. No, when I became Lady Savage I did not cook and I missed it. I'd done it, you see, when things turned sour at home when I was young. Before I was married. And I—" She came full stop, staring at him.

"You cooked for your parents?" Unusual. What did she mean, 'when things turned sour'?

"I did. My father lost his income. We were quite without funds. He was...inconsolable. My mother was...undone. She took to her bed and took her bottle of laudanum with her."

"Liv!"

"Oh, don't be sad. She'd always been moody. It was easy for me to take charge of one housemaid and I became the cook. When I was a child I'd spent so much time in the kitchen that returning to one, alone in peace and quiet, was a boon." She gave him a whimsical smile. "I was an only child and knew how to amuse myself in the kitchen, in my father's library or at the piano. I learned early the difference between being alone and being lonely."

"I'm sorry," he said. "I'm conjuring up awful memories."

"I don't mind recalling my past...or most of the time, I don't." She rallied, straightening her back against the squabs. She concentrated on the scenery. "You've reminded me of what I had to learn, what I had to endure. In times of peace, it's important to remember when you were in turmoil. When things were difficult and people were...unhappy. The past gives you perspective and hope."

He liked her positive attitude. "I agree. My own childhood was poor. Ireland then was no place for man or beast. Maybe it still isn't. My sister was rabid to leave. She saved her wages just to put us on a ship to America. And we both prospered. She waited tables in a pub near the docks of Baltimore and she made me go to school."

"I wondered how you became educated. How you went from a scrapper in the streets and lost your Irish brogue and learned about the sea and trade and railroads."

"It helps to be curious. I was. School fed my jumpy mind." Newspapers had made him famous. Gossip made him notorious. The first printed the truth. The last elaborated lies. For a woman to hear of his reputation seemed unusual, but Liv was in business herself, albeit it was true she was a noblewoman. "You had heard I was a boy from the streets, eh?"

She nodded. "I did. Many marvel at how you've done so very well financially."

"And socially?" He snorted, mocking himself. "I know many don't care for me."

"Ignore gossips," she said vehemently.

He frowned at her. "You pay them no mind? The gossips?"

"I try not to."

That didn't make sense. Why was she concerned about being seen with him if she dismissed those who told tales?

"But sometimes," she said with sorrow lining her brow, "I fail. But I tell myself they're mean. Of you? They're only jealous of your success. Or must compare themselves to feel superior. My father was like that. A needy man. Troubled. My mother, too. Looking for approval from those who couldn't give her the time of day. Did you like school?"

"I did." He pushed away his concern about her conflicting emotions. "I was all boy. Wanting to be out, dicing, fighting. So I hated a classroom at first. But when I skipped, my sister'd catch me and haul me right back by the ear. I learned to love my lessons and my sister's demands I learn."

"And where is she now? America?"

"She died more than fifteen years ago. But she had the good life she deserved, married to a man who was worthy of her. Hard-working and honest, he was."

"I like to hear of lives well lived," she said on a sigh. "My husband was such a man. He should have lived to a ripe old age. But he learned he had a...condition for which there was no cure. He suffered. So we had only eight years together."

"You miss him."

She met his gaze, and it took her a minute to respond. "He had his...foibles. But he was a fine man. So different from you."

That stung. He tried to ignore it, but couldn't.

She recoiled. "I didn't mean to be rude, Killian. Please don't take it that way."

He tried to brush it off. "Tell me how he was different."

"Oh, I—well..."

"I need to know." He pinned her with his gaze. "If you and I are to be friends, you must tell me."

"Yes." She bit her lower lip and fidgeted with the brim of her hat. Then she looked up at him. "He was thoughtful. Gentle and not at all—"

"What?"

"Aggressive. He'd never had to be. All that he had was inherited, given to him, nary a question as to his right to it. He was the most pleasant man to be near. Never fought. Never argued."

That sounded like a condemnation of Killian's own past, damning criticism of his own behavior. "I see."

She reached across the coach and took one of his hands. Neither of them had on their gloves and her skin was warm, her touch reassuring. "No, you don't."

"You consider me opposite of him?"

"In many ways, yes."

He could take umbrage at that. "But it's clear, my dear, that you loved him."

"Oh, I did. How could I not? He did save me from poverty and my family's poor reputation. He introduced me to the business of decorating. Showed me how to tell the authenticity of a Chippendale chair or Pugin's wallpaper. I can tell you if mahogany is from Honduras or Mexico and if the French polish on it merits the highest price. I owe him much." She had tears in her eyes.

He rose and sat beside her. Looping one arm around her shoulders, he drew her to him. "I've made you sad. I didn't mean to."

She nestled her face in the crook of his neck. Holding her was heaven. She was supple—and trusting.

He stroked her hair. "I'm glad to know you loved him. He sounds like he was a wonderful man and a good husband. He must have been exemplary to have gained your love."

She sniffed and pulled back. Her fingertips caressed his cheek. "You are a good man, too."

He dropped a kiss into her palm. "I learned to be."

She rested her head on his shoulder and gazed up at him. "How?"

"I fell in love with a woman who would bear no shenanigans from me. No cards. No dice. No fancy ladies."

"Your wife?"

He nodded once. "She helped me see that some actions of mine needed reforming. I needed, she said, principles."

"I like her."

"She was right. I...was lax in one negotiation. And the man suffered."

Liv went still. "How?"

"He died. Took his own life."

"You knew?" Her voice was a whisper of horror.

"I heard from my banker in London. After his death." Killian hated to recall it. "I force myself to recall the details. It keeps me...focused."

"And your wife knew?"

"I told her. I shared everything with her, especially my remorse over this."

"That's the way a marriage should be," she said with a watery smile.

He considered this woman in his arms, so sensitive and yet so strong. "I would have liked your husband."

She traced a fingertip along the outline of his lips. "And he would have liked you."

He caught a breath. Waited.

She cupped his jaw and with her eyes on his mouth, she put her lips to his. Her kiss was fierce and hot, a brief brand of frantic bliss.

She tore away.

He groaned and brought her more deeply into his embrace. She came so easily. His tongue danced with hers, ravenous. This is what he'd craved for weeks. This is who he'd wanted for months.

She pushed back, shock in her wide eyes. But in the next blink, she returned, her fingers sinking in his hair. This kiss was decadent fire.

He'd not known demand like this in ages. He kissed her once and again, stunned at her desire, mindless of his own, his whole body ablaze.

She broke away, panting. "This isn't supposed to happen."

"Why not, Liv?"

"Because you're different than I imagined."

"The gossips you reject labeled me one way—"

❧

"And you are quite another," she admitted.

Could she forgive him? Was her father's death the one that reformed him? If he had changed then, that was wonderful. But it hadn't changed her own life.

And to what extent was he responsible for that? Wasn't her father the one who bore responsibility for his own actions? His own decisions?

Yet, here she was face-to-face with a different man than the one she'd thought she hated. Certainly a different man from her husband.

He was dark, where her husband had been light. Blond, jovial, delicate David. As tall as she, slender, elegant. Agreeable. With nary a word of hate or anger. Lover of horses and dogs. Birds, too. He'd been as close to an angel any man could ever be. Too kind, too serene, he could not fight the disease that ate him from the inside out. He'd died as quietly as the morphine would allow, and on his lips praise for her, hope for her and rules to live by for Camille.

"Find a love to fill this void," he whispered to their young daughter who cried her eyes out that her precious papa was leaving them. "And help your mama to do the same."

Camille's promise to him had been one she quickly fulfilled for herself. Her writing was her insurance that what she loved, she'd do each day. Who she loved would come later. When Camille loved, she would choose a man on animal instinct and blind devotion.

But for Liv, no man had beckoned her to leave the walls of her self-imposed cloister. To emerge was to face society. A task she avoided if and when she could.

The memory of David and the way he had loved her so blithely rippled thought her like a fast-flowing stream. He had been gentle and wise. No commander of ships or savior of slaves. No conqueror of opponents. No tycoon of railroads and real estate. No wizard with money. No lover of women. But a lover of men.

This man who held her was the living, breathing, blood red opposite. Dark to light. Swift to slow. Bold to mellow, soft and sweet. A man who desired her.

The hackney rolled to a stop.

To have Killian, to possess the fire that he embodied, to fuel the flames of passion that sparked in her veins, she had to have him now. Here. In Brighton. In her sweet little house where no one else could say her nay. Or carry tales. Or ridicule her for her choice.

"Come inside with me."

Killian shook his head. "Liv..."

"Come inside." She put one finger to the corner of his firm and tempting mouth. "Don't you want to?"

"I came to Brighton to hold you, kiss you, but Liv, if I go inside your house..."

"I promise you'll come out intact," she said, hating that she sounded like she teased him. But she couldn't stop. Couldn't find seductive words. "I have brandy. No cigars, though, I'm afraid."

He gave a laugh and clutched her closer.

She needed him closer still, skin to her skin, heart to her heart. His lips were no longer enough.

"Liv, I'm not in the habit of having a lady for one night—"

He was refusing her? Her whole body ached with the loss. He feared she would trap him? No, he couldn't. And she wouldn't. "Killian, I'm not young. Not a debutante in search of a beau. Or a husband."

He circled his big hand around the back of her neck and spoke on her lips. "I want you for yourself, but not—"

"Forgive me." She jerked away, gathered her little reticule and her straw hat, then got to her feet to leave the carriage. At that moment, the coachman pulled open the door. "Thank you for the day, Killian. I must go. Monday, I'd say, we see the draper on Water Street."

He snatched her hand.

She shook him off. On unsteady feet, she marched the three steps to her little portico. In the light of the gas lamps, she fished her latch key from her reticule. Her lower lip quivered so badly, she had to bite it. Fumbling, she fit the key in and pushed open the door.

A vise circled round her, her breath left her lungs. An arm to her waist, another under her knees, and suddenly she was off her feet, in his arms and inside. Killian had her and with a foot, he slammed her front door closed. The sound reverberated in her little hall.

She grinned at him.

"I presume we're climbing the stairs?" he asked her with a tinge of anger and a hint of the rogue.

"We are," she said tightening her arm around his shoulder. "I can walk."

"Like hell you will."

"I'm heavy," she declared as he took the stairs up and she thrust her arms around his massive shoulders.

"I'm not letting you go," he bit off the words as he trudged upward.

"You'll sprain your back. Then where will we be? Not in bed."

"Trust me, my lady." He took the last two steps up. "That's where we're going."

He stood in the hall, looking from one closed door to the other. "Which?"

She pointed.

"Open it."

She giggled and turned the handle.

He pushed it open with a shoulder and whirled her inside to press her against the wall.

CHAPTER 13

"Now," he whispered to her as he cupped her face, "we're here. You're mine. And before I take all these clothes from you, I need to kiss you once more."

"Why is that?" She spoke on his lips, her body lush and limp against the length of his own.

"Because I need to feel all of you. Soft as butter in my hands." He stroked her throat, her shoulders. "I want you melting."

Her eyes drifted closed. Her mouth fell open. "I've been a puddle of impatience since you first looked at me."

He laughed, but nothing was funny about the hard points of her nipples against his thumbs. Or the way she rubbed one leg up his and hooked it around his thigh. "I've wanted my hands on you, all over you—"

"No time," she whispered on a moan, circling her arms around his waist. "Now, now. I've waited too long."

So have I. "But rushing you would be a crime."

She ground her teeth. "Cursed man."

Chuckling, he cupped her shoulders and turned her to the

wall. "I hate buttons," he said as he dispensed with hers. Her gown slid to the floor.

"And tabs." He tore open the one at her petticoat and as it pooled at her feet, he worked at the ties. "I vote that women discard bustles and drawers."

"And corsets?" she asked laughing at she whirled to face him.

In the rays from the street lamplights, he admired her perfect skin, elegant shoulders, her rounded breasts...her naked hips and long lean thighs. He gulped, frantic, a boy with his first lover.

She was attired only in her frilly white corset, her nude femininity covered in a froth of auburn hair, and the long suspenders from her corset that held up her fine white stockings. He swallowed the lump in his throat at how damn curvaceous she was. How he was going to love every inch of her.

He set to work on the ties that bound up her breasts while she unhooked her garters. When he peeled the corset away, all air left his chest. Her breasts—round firm healthy orbs—were the loveliest he'd ever seen. Her nipples, too, were lovely, large, hard pink nubs. He put his palms up, but his hands shook. He checked her eyes.

She considered him, her lips open, her gaze yearning, her back to the wall, her hands flat against the plaster. "Do you like me?"

"Like?" He wasn't sure that was his voice. "A weak word, 'like'."

She tipped her head, sweet and sultry.

He stepped to her, stroking her arms, her hands, her bare belly, her sleek hip. He was so eager, he might fail to love her as slowly as she merited.

"I'm going to be a dead man soon. Just looking at you stops my heart."

Her mouth formed an O and she murmured his name.

But he couldn't move, couldn't help himself. He stared at her. He'd look at her until he was an old man, who was, because of her, horny as the devil. She was so luscious, a curvy woman with those fabulous breasts. He was going to lick them, suck them and cry in joy. Those round hips. He was going to caress them, mold them to his own and live for minutes after as a satyr. But her mound, her curly red hair. He was going to pet her, part her folds, lave her, suck her into his mouth and submerge himself in all she was. He was going to love her in the flesh because—*oh, Killian Hanniford, you crazy scoundrel*—he loved her.

For that, he had no words yet. But soon, he'd tell her. And for now, there was just this. "I hope I can do you justice."

She writhed back against the wall with a feline confidence that seemed new, borne just for him. "I don't doubt it. But really, darling, you must hurry."

He snorted, put his hands over her marvelous breasts and bent to bless each nipple with a tender kiss. "The last thing we need is speed."

She hung lax and dolorous in his arms. "If you don't hurry, I may dissolve right here."

He chuckled. "No, you won't. You want my mouth on you here." He drew one nipple into his mouth, bit her, and then sucked the other one in, and teased her with his tongue.

"You want my hands on you here," he said and stroked down her ribs and around her buttocks to lift her and press her to his raging erection.

She swallowed hard and loud, as she dug her nails into his shoulders.

"And here," he gruffed as he sent his flat palm down her belly to the wealth of her hair, "you want my fingers." He parted her lips where she was soaked. "You want my praise for how well you show you want me." He sank his fingers inside her to caress her silken inner walls. As she mewled, he kissed her ear. "My darling, you need me and I am yours."

She reeled.

But with one hand to her hip, he pressed her to the wall as he sank to his knees and urged her to widen her legs. In the dim light streaming in the window, he detected her beauty. Her thighs were muscular, shapely, her bush trim. Her pale folds fragrant with desire for him. With two fingers, he spread her lips and she moaned, thrashed her head against the wall, but he soothed her with a stroke.

"I will taste you and love you and you'll stand there and let me. You'll love it because you need this and I must have all of you in every way I can."

She gave a little cry.

And he sank to her sweet lips. She was so silky, so musky, so enchanting in her surrender to him. He put his mouth on her and let his tongue love her. Opening her wider, he found her nub and kissed her, then sucked her up. She quaked, her climax wild and loud.

She sank in his arms. "Killian, please!"

He spread her out beneath him. His naked prize for being patient. He stroked her hair and cuddled her close. She shook, her sounds of completion joy to his ears and her vibrations long and lovely to his eyes.

Quiet, replete, she stroked a fingertip over his lower lip. "That was beyond words."

"It was," he said, thrilled at her unbridled response to him. He'd not tasted a woman like that in years. So many years. Since his wife's death, he'd taken women for a night or mistresses for a month or even a few. But he'd not wanted this intimate possession. With Liv on his lips, he filled with a madness to have her again like that. But first, he'd fill himself and her with the power of a mutual mating. He'd savor her with his cock.

He got to his feet and pulled her up with him. "Come to bed, my lady. We've more to do here."

She rose to him, a torrid grin on her face. Her hands to his stock, his shirt, his vest, she peeled his frock coat from his shoulders. "I want to see your skin. Your nipples." She cupped him in his trousers. "Very impressive. I want all of this, you wicked man."

He laughed and disrobed as efficiently as he could, given her continuing caress of his very hard and tender penis. "Darling, you'd better take your hands off me."

She rubbed her hand along the length of him.

He caught her wrist and stayed her moves. Coughing, he said, "If you want me inside you, sweetheart, don't make me come in your hand."

As if burned, she pulled back. Then she strolled to her little bed and whirled to face him. Waggling a finger, she indicated his form. "Now, Hanniford. I'm getting cold."

He stripped out of his clothes like a man on fire. Naked, he let her look.

Slapping a hand to her heart, she stared at him. "Oh," was all she could seem to manage.

He stepped to her, took her hand and put it around him.

"Oh," was her only word.

He leaned over her, stroked one of her satin nipples and sank a finger up inside her succulent hot core.

"Oh, oh."

He picked her up and urged her more fully on the bed. There, he stretched out beside her to nibble on her breasts and bite her fingertips, smooth the expanse of her flat belly and delve inside her thick wet folds to find her center and roll her nub until she cried out, clutching him once more.

"You're a terrible man," she said as she quivered in her joy of him.

"I can tell," he said with a smug satisfaction and a raging need to plunge inside her.

"Come, have me, darling." She urged him over her. "Please, please."

At once, he froze.

She pecked him on the mouth. "What's wrong?" she begged him like a tormented girl.

"Liv, darling?" Reality burned his mind. Through the euphoria of his lust for her, in the admission of his love for her, he had forgotten one basic rule.

She frowned, her sweet eyes filled with fear. "What?"

"If there's a baby—"

"No," she smiled sweetly at him, her hips undulating against his in invitation. "There won't be."

He would not shame her. He loved her. He'd marry her. "You can't be sure."

❧

She did not move for a long minute, considering the severity of the subject. "I'm thirty-eight. I've not had a regular monthly in ages and after Camille was born, I was never with child." He didn't need to know why. She reached up and brushed her lips on his. His mouth held the flavors of her body. To savor them on a man's lips for the first time was a rousing and titillating experience. "You can't leave me now. Not after you've tasted me."

He tucked her under him, his massive body covering her with warm and wild desire. "I want you. Wanted you for so long."

"No man," she said, quivering with excitement, "has ever said that to me."

"I'll repeat it," he whispered, his lips skimming her own, "and become all men to you."

Gasping, she tilted up her hips and detected the tip of his cock. He was a huge man, larger than she thought a man could be. But then, she'd had David only a few times and his penis had flagged quickly. They'd coupled quickly and without much in the way of kisses or caresses. He'd done what he must to seal their vows. Her knowledge of men was so limited.

These raptures she felt in Killian's embrace were addictive. That she would not deny. If that was lust, then she also doubted she'd never find such enjoyment with any other man. This one was too endearing. Unique. A lover she could savor, body and soul. And she was ravenous to have him fill her, make her pulse with the power of his thrusts. "Come inside me."

He inched into her core. She panted, eager, desperate. She put a hand to his firm ass and pressed down. "Have me, Hanniford. I'm not glass and, God knows, I burn to have you."

With one long slow glide, his gaze holding hers, he slid into her full bore. She arched up, her whole body ardent, seeking, filled to the brim with this man.

This man who was bigger than others. This legend, who was mightier than many. This tycoon, scoundrel, wicked thief of her heart. And she loved him.

Adored him.

How he made love to her. How he cared for her. Held her hand. Chided her. Wiped her tears. Made her laugh.

He paused, caught her chin. "Look at me. Where are you?"

"Here, here," she assured him. Her admission of her love pushed aside, thrown away from this moment in her mind, she flowed with him. His cock took her up and she reveled in him.

He plunged into her with precision, drove her up up up to

oblivion and frantic, rocking bliss. She shook and he came with a growl and sharp thrusts. She took them all, savored the harshness of his rise and the sweetness of his fall. For long minutes, he covered her and she welcomed the weight, the fervor, the claim of him.

He rolled to one side and left her empty. Even though he combed her hair from her eyes, she noted the lack of him.

"I prefer you inside me."

"If I stayed, I'd crush you."

She laughed. "I'll have to be on top next time."

He sank his fingers into her hair and kissed her with a hearty smack. "I'm glad to hear there will be a next time."

She wiggled her brows. "Soon?"

"Is there a time limit?"

"Do I have enough to go get you that brandy I offered?"

"That depends."

"On?"

He ran a hand over one of her nipples and circled his thumb over it. "You grow hard quickly, darling. You'd better not be gone too long, wouldn't you say?"

She snuggled closer. "Perhaps if you give me incentive."

He gave her a singular arched look. "To go or stay?"

"Stay."

He grinned, then pushed her to her back and put his mouth over her breast. His tongue was the most talented organ in England.

In minutes, she was writhing in his arms, his mouth on one nipple, her flesh pounding over his skillful fingers. And then he curled her against him and stroked her back as if she were a cat.

Against her tummy, she felt the hard probe of his cock and smiled. "Perhaps I should go now for your brandy?"

"Perhaps you'd prefer to stay a few minutes?"

Breathless, she propped herself up on one arm, her mouth

watering at the sight of his very ripe interest. She lay her hand on his length and the girth of him, the heat of him pulsing through her. "I think you'll wait for that brandy."

Minutes later, she rolled to her back, threw her arms over her head, grinned at him and sighed. In the eight years she'd been married, she'd had no rippling moments of fulfillment. In fact, Camille's conception had been a huge shock to both David and her. Truly, in the last hour, she could count more sexual satisfaction than she'd enjoyed in all her life.

But her next thought caused a lump in her throat. She'd never before been consumed by such blinding passion for a man. And much as she'd loved him, not ever for her husband.

⊗

Killian rose from her bed as he saw a ray of sun dart through the gray clouds beyond her bedroom window. Losing the heat of her body shocked his system, but he padded over to her draperies and spread the heavy damask wide. From here he saw down to the coast where a few dark figures walked the rocky shore.

Liv looped her arms around his waist, her lips to his spine. "I must go."

He heard her moan. "Don't. Stay."

He turned in her embrace. "Aren't you concerned someone will know?"

"No." She kissed him full on the mouth and he yearned to return the homage. "I have a maid-of-all-work but I gave her a half day yesterday and whole today. She's gone to Hove to visit her family and won't be here until tomorrow morning. Stay with me, Killian. Let me cook for you. I'll play the piano too."

He hugged her close. "You have a piano here?"

"I rented one from a local seller." She widened her eyes,

playful as he'd not seen her before. "Chopin? Bach? Bacon and cheese with eggs? What is your pleasure?"

"You know the answer to that last," he said and squeezed her luscious body against his.

"Wonderful." She tore away and danced backwards. "Would you like a robe?"

He knit his brows. "Silk?"

With a flourish of one hand, she indicated his face. "A wonderful fine weave from Chinese worms. Red and yellow butterflies. It'll compliment your complexion."

"Like hell it will. Thank you, I'll wash up and dress."

Her face fell. "What a shame."

He chuckled. "You won't dress?"

She preened, then crossed her arms. Her breasts swelled and her nipples beckoned him. "Do I need to?"

"A robe, oh tempting one. At the very least."

She strolled away. The sight of her derriere as she flexed her muscles made him rethink his suggestion of some garment.

He groaned. "I'm dressing. Where's a pitcher? I'll go out to the pump and get wash water."

She was shrugging into a yellow silk robe and tying the sash beneath her breasts. "You're a darling. The pump is out back. I'll show you the way and the pitcher is...here." She took a large blue china one from behind her dressing screen.

"I'll put on clothes and go out," he grumbled as he pulled on his undergarment and his pants. "One thing I'll treasure in this new house will be the indoor plumbing."

She waltzed over, rose on her toes and planted a kiss on his cheek. "A man of the future!"

The question was, was he a man in *her* future?

The next morning before dawn as he climbed out of her bed and pushed the curtain aside, he had a partial answer. He was a man she enjoyed. A man she desired. Often and with unbridled pleasure. But he wouldn't make her his mistress. And he had to go slowly to ensure she welcomed all he would offer her.

The sun had not yet risen but the wind off the coast was strong, battering the window panes. He crawled back into her bed beside her with gratitude for her warmth. She snuggled up to him.

"Now I must leave."

She wiggled her hips against his. "I wish you didn't have to."

He turned in her embrace. Her hair tousled, her eyelids drowsy with fatigue, naked, she was a carefree insistent lover luring him like a siren.

"No. I must." All too aware of her sensitivity to be seen with him, he didn't want to aggravate the issue by leaving her home in broad daylight. If they were to continue their affair, how long could they keep it secret? He didn't want to. God knew, he wanted more of her, perhaps all of her forever. But if she was ashamed of him, his name, his reputation, his past, their love affair would necessarily be short and for him, bittersweet. He wasn't a man to play a waiting game. His entire life and his business success had been built on instinct, speed and decisiveness. In love, he would not change. Could not. He'd force the matter...and do it now. "You know it's best I do."

She tried to smile, but it was a watery expression. "Do you still want to go to the drapers?"

"I do." *Do you?*

She nodded. "Can I make you tea before you leave?"

"No."

She burrowed into him, her ferocity to hold him contrast to her dislike of being seen with him.

He moved away from her, picking up his clothes.

She donned her robe that she'd flung over the bed and sat on the edge to watch him as he dressed. She was silent.

He formed a plan.

Securing the last button on his frock coat, he went to her and raised her chin with two fingers. "I'll return at ten o'clock. When I do, I want an answer."

"To what?" She looked wary, surprised.

"I want you to come to Paris with me. Tomorrow. It will be business. You'll stay at the Grand Hotel. I'll be at Boulevard Haussmann. Pierce is there finalizing a few of his own business contracts. You and I will go to the silk merchants and the art agent who sells Marianne's and Remy's pieces. I have an invitation to a soirée at the home of a French financier. Pierce has accepted for himself. But I want you to come with me. And I plan a dinner party. I'd like you to be my hostess."

She said nothing for a very long time, her face a sea of emotions from shock to sadness to the utter fascination she'd worn when she was in his arms this past day and a half. "I've not been in society for many years. I'm not certain I'd be your finest hostess."

He waited, his heart sinking. She was refusing him. The only woman who'd mesmerized him in decades.

"If I go with you and find I cannot do it, you must promise me to let me return here without objection."

She gave him fragile hope. Whereas he must give her assurance. "You must be with me because you want to, Liv. I'd have you no other way."

She got to her feet and pulled him close. "I find that I need you, Killian. I'll gladly come."

CHAPTER 14

Place du Tertre
Montmartre, Paris

"You look wonderfully rested," Liv told Marianne as she kissed her on both cheeks. Two happy people, the duc de Remy and his duchesse of only eight months looked sun-kissed in their informal white summer clothes.

"Andre insists I go to bed every hour!" Marianne's green eyes twinkled as she cast her husband a grin and went to embrace her uncle Killian. "He is a pest!"

"The rest works," Killian said as he hugged his niece. "How about you, Remy? Any sleep?"

The tall blond Frenchman clasped Killian's hand. "Very little."

Liv and Killian had taken the train from London to Paris two days ago. The holiday with Killian proved a whirlwind of delights. Dining alone with him in noisy, fragrant, sumptuous restaurants. Attending the theatre, thrilled at his taste, his looks, the way other women glanced at him and tossed her knowing glances of appreciation. Walking with him once more under the stars. Every moment was a delight.

"The two nurses he hired are excellent," Marianne put in as the four took chairs around the little table on the veranda of the restaurant. "But he insists on supervising their every move. So, no, Uncle Killian, Andre is haggard. Not completing his latest work."

A playful smile on his face, Killian tsked. "Which is what?"

"I'm sculpting a piece I attempted over a year ago. I was dissatisfied with it."

"Oh? What?" Liv asked, grateful for the shade of the plane trees in the square. In their corner of the restaurant's terrace, the view to the plaza was limited and she gave herself over to enjoying the company of her cousin, his wife and Killian.

"A baby," the new father said with a silly grin.

Killian laughed. "Re-doing a piece in your new son's image?"

"He's very good looking," Marianne said with a wink.

"Well, I understand your pride," Liv said recalling her own joy in the birth of Camille. She'd never even thought she could get pregnant and her daughter was a present God had granted her to brighten her existence. "Babies are such fun."

"Rand is the happiest child," Marianne said, a hand to her ribcage, grimacing and looking for a moment very uncomfortable. "No trouble at all. Our nurses are unemployed."

"Are you in pain?" Remy asked her, worry creasing his broad brow.

"No, no, *mon cher*. It's the corset. You know I hate it."

Remy took his wife's hand and held tightly to her. "This is why we don't go out for long. Her labor lasted more than ten hours. She's not ready yet to venture out."

"But I insisted," Marianne was quick to add. "Don't be

alarmed, Uncle Killian. If we didn't come out today, I was going to escape my bedroom by sliding down the bed sheets through the window."

Liv laughed. "And getting out is good for you. Remy, you mustn't badger her to remain indoors. The sun is glorious today. Besides, we won't detain you."

The waiter appeared and Remy acknowledged him by name. "A bottle of champagne, Cartot. Five glasses as we expect one more person."

"*Oui, Monsieur le duc*." He nodded and trotted away.

"So you're calling our Bertrand, Rand?" Killian asked the couple.

"I like it," said Marianne with a toss of her pale blond curls. "Andre's mother prefers his full name."

"And I," said Remy, "avoid any controversy and call him *mon grand.*"

"I can't wait to see him. He's big, eh?" Liv asked.

Remy winced. "And long."

"In those ten hours I pushed to give him birth, I could have sworn," Marianne said with eyes going wide as saucers, "he weighed as much as Remy."

Killian chuckled.

Liv said, "Babies always feel like that as you give birth, until you hold them in your arms and marvel at how infinitely tiny they are."

Marianne got a funny smile on her face. "Rand will be a giant like his father."

"And a sculptor as well?" Liv asked Remy.

"Or a painter like his mother," Remy said. "Whatever he wishes is what he shall become. I've no rule. Freedom is best."

"Agreed," said Killian. "I didn't expect Pierce to become interested in business. In fact, he was off to a slow start, but now he's adding to our company with steel contracts here in

France. He's also a valuable advisor on the new plumbing we're doing in the townhouses we've planned in Brighton."

"And you are recommending the interior designs for them and for Killian's new house, aren't you, Liv?" Marianne asked.

"I am. In fact, the reason I'm here is to help Killian choose a few good items."

"Including," added Killian as the waiter appeared with their glasses and champagne, "paintings and sculpture I'd like for my long gallery."

Marianne grinned at him. "Just like a fine English lord."

"Or an American one," Killian added while the *garçon* poured their wine.

"That's why we want you to meet Edouard Montand," Remy said to him. "He can tell you whose works are selling and why. Degas, Renoir, Sisley, Manet."

"First," Killian said as he fingered the base of his crystal flute, "I wish to buy a Duquesne and a Remy."

Liv smiled as each of them shot back in their chairs.

"No," said Marianne.

"Absolutely not," echoed Remy.

"You will not *buy* a thing."

"Marianne," Killian objected.

She put up a hand. "Uncle, I am here because you have been kind to me. All my life."

"And I am here, Killian, because I love the niece you cared for. Do not think we would take money from you for anything."

Liv sat back, sipping her champagne as the three of them argued, politely but hotly, over money.

"After you meet Edouard and we finish," Remy said, "we'll walk over to our studio and you will choose whatever you wish."

"As our gifts," Marianne said.

"I do not intend to take—"

"You're not *taking* anything, Uncle Killian." Marianne reached out and squeezed his hand.

"I'll choose a small piece—"

Marianne scowled at him. "You're being stubborn."

"Besides, Killian, if you choose something insignificant, Marianne and I will simply choose pieces for you. The bigger, the better."

Marianne nodded. "There you have it. Now argue with us."

"One condition."

"Name it," Remy said.

"When I buy a piece from your friends, you will not tell any of them who I am or encourage them or your agent to sell me anything for a pittance."

"All of our friends, Uncle Killian, are very poor. We urge you to pay more than the asking price for whatever you like."

Liv chuckled. "I've been witness to that. Don't argue with him is my suggestion."

Killian grinned. "If you do, I'll drive the value of all their works higher."

Marianne sat back and clapped her hands. "That you will. Instantly."

"*Bonjour, Madame la duchesse, et Monsieur le duc.*"

Standing beside Liv was an older, elegant man of middling height, ample girth, with a substantial winged mustache, pointed goatee and the sharp eyes of a man about town. He bowed over Marianne's hand and kissed it, then allowed Remy to introduce him to her and Killian. But Liv could only nod woodenly. The art agent, *Monsieur* Montand, had a friend.

And she knew him. Knew him well.

"Allow me to present a friend of mine," said Montand. "We met here in the square just as I alighted from my cab. He seeks pieces he might take home to Gloucester to decorate his home. I told him I was to meet you, *Madame* and *Monsieur*, so of course he insisted on being introduced."

"Forgive the intrusion," said Lord Horace Mayhew who had been a close friend of her husband's. They'd gone to Eton as well as done their grand tour together. His large brown eyes rested in hers. "Lady Savage and I are well acquainted. How are you, Olivia?"

"Very well, Horace." She allowed him to take her hand and kiss it. "Delightful to see you again."

"And you. It's been many years."

Since you came to David's funeral. "Indeed. You're looking well."

"Thank you. As are you."

He'd been truly happy to see her until the next moment when Remy introduced him to Killian.

"Killian Hanniford. Why, how wonderful to meet you, sir." But his words were stiff and his smile thin.

He recognizes Killian's name and the connection.

She wished to dissolve in her chair.

He knows I shouldn't be here with him.

They conversed about the heat, the artists working in the plaza and then Remy invited Mayhew to join them for luncheon.

Liv held her breath.

"No, *merci beaucoup,* I must go." He absently fingered his delicate watch fob dangling from his waistcoat pocket, but his eyes flew time and again to Liv's. "My wife is at Worth's and I'm to meet her there in an hour. You know how that is. I must go to pay the bill."

He bid them all *adieu* in the most pleasant terms. He'd always been a kind man.

But his wife? Oh, Liv knew his wife. That woman was not kind. She was a creature of the *ton*. Addicted to her clothes, her jewels, her houses, even her lovers. Those last—and numerous they'd been, too—made up for the lack in her husband's affections. For Mayhew preferred men. Men like David.

"Come sit, Edouard," Remy welcomed his friend and agent. "We've a glass ready for you."

"And we're delighted to say," said Marianne," that my uncle prepares to buy whatever you tell him will be the next sensation."

Liv sat back, her heart pounding, her fears doubling that her time with Killian was very short. Shorter than she predicted. Because the fear in her heart spread like poison through her bloodstream. Listening with half a heart, half an ear, half a mind, she took part in the discussion when she could with a smile and a nod.

But her flesh crawled as she imagined Mayhew climbing the staircase in the House of Worth on the Rue de la Paix and mulling over what he'd just witnessed. His wife, curse her, would notice his confusion and ask its source. He'd never been clever or wily. Always an open gregarious creature whom David had loved with every ounce of his uncomplicated soul. Mayhew would casually tell her that the most extraordinary thing just happened when he was up in Montmartre. Of all people, he'd run into Olivia Bereston.

You remember her, he'd say.

His wife would fix her ferret's eyes on him, widening her nostrils. "David's widow?"

Yes. And would you believe, I saw her with that notorious American? That Killian Hanniford.

"Hanniford? You don't say."

I do.

"The one who bankrupted her father?" she'd scoff.

Quite so.

"Why he killed himself? Wasn't it?"

CHAPTER 15

On their journey through the streets of Paris down from Montmartre, Liv found no words. Traffic was brisk and Killian's coachman arrived at the Grand Hotel within minutes. Liv tried not to twist her gloves to ropes, but she couldn't stop, couldn't look at Killian. He finally moved to her side of the carriage and took her in his arms. She welcomed his solace, even though she owed him an explanation.

He didn't ask. Sweet man.

He was so wise. That was how he'd survived and prospered throughout his life.

She was grateful. Coward that she was.

When his town coach idled before the entrance to the hotel, instead of remaining inside, Killian got out. "Return in an hour, Robert."

If he walked through the lobby and followed her upstairs, everyone would see he was her lover.

But, what did it matter?

Shame washed through her. Shame of her father. Her mother. Her husband. All their choices.

She picked up her skirts and marched inside. Everyone would learn soon enough. Courtesy of Alice, Lady Horace Mayhew.

Liv took the central stairs. Her rooms on the third floor overlooked the grand circle entrance to the Opera and she loved standing at the tall French windows watching the patterns of the hackneys and coaches, the omnibuses and the lorries. All hours of the day and night, they went round and round in an endless symphony of sound. She liked the synchronicity of it, as if the muffled notes were meant to be, inevitable and unemotional. She loved to stand her back against the open panes and let in the breezes and the sounds of their infinite rounds.

She opened her door and Killian walked in close behind her. She threw down her little purse and parasol on a hall chair and continued through her sitting room to her bedroom.

Standing before her chiffonier, she put her hands on her hips, her back to him. "Please undo me."

She could hear him behind her, removing his coat, undoing his cufflinks and dropping them with two clinks to the bedside table. This would be their last minutes of intimacy.

She felt the tug of his hands on her gown. A bit rough—angry most likely—he continued his pursuit of her buttons and hooks, her laces and tabs. Naked, her clothes a gaudy pile of fabric around her feet, she waited for his caresses. Today, she needed them, all of them. Long, fervent, enthralling strokes that he lavished on her, proving to her over and over that she belonged to him. At least for that moment, for the afternoon.

Today, he took an extraordinarily long time and she couldn't object. He smoothed both his palms down her throat and blessed her nape with a torrid kiss. She leaned back into his embrace, allowing him to spread his legs and support her this one last time. He circled his arms around her and cupped each breast, thumbing her nipples until she moaned, her lower body flooding with need and crying out at the emptiness that had to be filled by him and soon.

He splayed his fingers down her ribcage and sent one hand down to her mound where he sank into her hair and found her center. There, he pressed his hand to her hot and needy core and bit her on the shoulder.

She tried to turn, but he clamped her to him like a vise. "Let me do this for you."

And there in the middle of her carpet, he massaged her and petted her until she whimpered in ecstasy and her knees buckled under her.

He caught her up and led her to the bed where he laid her out as if she were his pagan prize, climbed up between her thighs and kissed her to a high and fulfilled keen.

"Take these off," she yanked at his cravat and his shirt. "I need you."

He stood away from her and dispensed with his clothes, his silver gaze caressing her face and naked form. Unbuttoning his trousers, he let them fall but fished something from his pocket, then joined her on the bed. With a hand under each of her knees, he pulled her legs up and pushed her ankles back. There he licked her to another erotic explosion and finally settled above her and dropped into her.

He was fire and she was swollen desire. And with a madness only he could conjure in her, he brought her to a new and sweeter plain, this climax as wild as any of the others. He drifted down over her and held her tightly. She was his possession and she reveled in it one last time.

Cooler, sated, she pulled back and gave him a smile of gratitude. She made to leave him, but he pressed her shoulder to the mattress.

"As we are now, is how we were meant to be."

Her heart cracked open. Now the argument would begin. He'd ask what it was about Horace that had frozen her. She'd have to tell him everything. What a coward she'd been. What a mess her life had been. How she'd decided to meet him, gone purposely to Elanna's wedding only out of curiosity and meanness. Gone to Remy's and Marianne's because she had to reconfirm how infuriating her attraction to him was. How errant her sexual attraction to him. How unethical her need to see him smile at her, flirt and pursue her. Revenge hadn't even been her motive, because how could she, insignificant as she was, hurt the magnificent wealthy tycoon, Black Irish Hanniford?

"Liv, sweetheart." He placed a tender kiss on her lips. His body still joined with hers, he undulated inside her to bring her attention to him. "Listen to me. Look at me."

She saw him through the haze of her rapture and her pain.

"Liv, I love you."

She stared at him. She'd known it, of course, she had. He wore his love like a sheen of light. An aura in which he always enfolded her.

But he mustn't care for her.

"Liv," he whispered and caressed her cheek with the backs of his fingers. "My darling, I love you."

She shook herself to some sensitive response. "Killian, no, you don't. This is lust. This is—"

"Love." He shifted, still inside her deep and hot, but he brought forth into her view a huge ring of gold with tiny diamonds and one central ruby. "Marry me, Liv."

Her mouth fell open and she worked at words. Crazed, frantic, afraid she would laugh hysterically, she gasped. For him to love her was pure irony. For him to marry her would be ludicrous.

She shook her head. And this time, when she moved to slide out from under him, he let her go.

From the rumpled coverlet and sheets, he sat propped up on one elbow with his gaze boring into hers. "Now tell me what happened up there this afternoon and why that means you won't marry me."

"I know him."

"Clearly."

"He was a friend of my husband's." To go on was to walk into the limbo she'd lived in with David. To tell Killian all, was to open the door to the nightmare she'd lived most of her life.

Killian set his jaw and slid from the bed. Walking around, he gathered his clothes and jerked them on. When he was in his shirt, his waistcoat hanging open, his trousers secured, he strode to her liquor cart. With a few brisk moves, he poured two glasses full of brandy and handed her one. Then he took a seat in the boudoir chair that faced her. One leg crossed over the other, he focused on her with the intensity for which he'd been prized and ridiculed all these years.

He would not move. He wanted answers. And she couldn't blame him, even if she hated that she had to confess them.

Self-conscious at her nudity, she put down the glass and went to her wardrobe and removed her silk robe. It was too sheer, clinging to her curves and much too risqué for the conversation they were about to have, but she had no time to look for something more demure. Facing him, she tied the sash beneath her breasts, picked up her glass and downed a large swallow. She'd need courage for this. If she had it from a bottle, so be it.

"I cannot marry you because we are not suited."

He swirled the brandy in his glass. "You've tried that line. We've proved that wrong."

Very well. "I told myself I would never marry again."

He did not blink one eyelash.

She whipped out an arm. "I don't like belonging to someone."

He took a drink and savored it as his quicksilver eyes narrowed on her.

"I don't like having someone overshadow me. People thinking, assuming things about me that aren't true. Could never be true."

He wasn't going to speak. He was going to sit there stoic as a prophet until kingdom come and let her rave on.

"*Oh, God!* He was David's lover."

Killian's lips parted.

"My husband was a homosexual. He'd known it since he was sent off to school. Horace was one of his lovers. Not the only one, but the one who was the most regular. And Horace was kind to David. He kept reappearing whenever my husband had a financial loss or he suffered estate problems or crop failures. He'd often pay his bills, *our* bills, until David and I began to advise on home interior decoration and earn our keep."

Killian studied her, compassion softening the thin line of his mouth.

She loathed it. The sympathy.

Groaning, she turned away to pace and drink and drain her glass.

"I hated that people knew. As if I were less a woman. He less a man. I despised those who sneered at me and him. He was a kind man, gentle, sweet really. He married me because—"

That brought her up short. She faced Killian, fury from

her past ablaze with hatred and sorrow for what she had been.

"He married me because he felt sorry for me. We'd been friends since childhood and we got on well. I knew what he was. I was his respectable wife even though my family was not...not without shame. We were poor, my family was so awfully poor after...after my father lost his wealth. My mother became an addict to laudanum. Living in her own sweet oblivion, she had no care for any of us. Not Father, not me. She was quite insane. We had to put her in restraints so that she wouldn't bite her flesh and chew her hands off."

"Oh, sweetheart."

"No!" She seethed and slashed the air with one hand. "No. I won't have your pity. I don't need it. You take it back."

He winced, concern lining his brow.

"Oh, that's what I am now to you. As crazy as she was?" She inhaled and cinched her sash tighter. "Well, I'm not. I'm stronger than that. Than she was. And that's why—"

He cocked his head.

"Why I value my independence. What I do is for me and for Camille. I make my own reputation. Not live off any man's."

He blanched.

"I had to live in the shadow of my father's. The shadow of David's. I won't live in yours, either."

He cursed, a whisper of incredulity. "You are ashamed of me."

She stepped toward him. "*What?* Are you mad?"

He shot from his chair and plunked the glass on the table. Approaching her, he stood before her and crossed his massive arms. "I've noted when we're out together how you search for anyone you might know. You're afraid, Liv, of anyone seeing you with me. And today, far from home, that man recognized you."

"Yes." She admitted it. *Damn the truth.*

His jaw worked. His eyes lost their glitter. He dropped his arms to his sides and ran a weary hand through his hair. He whirled, picked up his frock coat and headed for the door.

She raced to him to grab his arm. More words—more horrifying words—clogged in her throat.

He shook her off but looked down at her, his face white. "I can't change who I was. The same as you can't change your past. But I've tried. So have you. Still you don't see it. But think on this: Over the years, one thing I have learned is that love can do a damn sight more to make us happy than pride ever could."

"I am proud of you. But it's not pride that made me refuse you."

"What then?"

She wrung her hands. "Fear. Failure to tell you the truth."

"So then," he drew near with anger in his words, "you trust me with your body...and perhaps even your heart, but not with the truth?"

"Oh, Killian!" She clenched her fists in a rage of sorrow. "My maiden name is Emley. Emley."

He went white. Only his eyes searched the room, her family name a silent repetition on his lips.

She could not bear to watch him absorb the tragedy of it. "Please go."

"No." He reached for her.

She avoided him and hurried to the door. She whirled to face him "Now."

He stared at her. Then at once, as if electrified, he strode toward her. "We will talk about this."

She opened the door. "Talk changes nothing."

"It's the *only* thing that changes people." He strode right up to her, his hands clutching her shoulders. "I told you once that the past was a landscape I could not change. I won't try.

But we can have a future—and I can make that bright." He pulled her close, kissed the crown of her head.

But she stepped backward.

"Very well. We are not done."

"We were finished before we began."

"No. I only hope we have enough years left so that I can make amends for all the pain I caused you. I will ensure, my darling, that you let me try."

CHAPTER 16

The morning after her return from Paris, Liv sent around a note to Roger Antram. She wished to see him in his offices the next afternoon at one o'clock.

Liv had debated writing to him to notify him she wished an appointment, afraid he'd inform Killian and ask him to attend, too. But she had no idea if Killian had returned yet from Paris. His scheduled dinner party for business associates in Paris was to occur tonight. She doubted he'd cancel it. Certainly not to chase her home, he wouldn't. Shouldn't. What point would there be in that? She'd rejected him.

It was only fitting she face Roger soon. He'd been too kind to her since David's death, helping her to build her reputation as a solo decorator and expanding her clientele. Her husband had valued Roger and their relationship had always been upright, honest and profitable, too. She couldn't simply resign her association with him by letter. That would be an insult. Plus she had to lay out for him what she'd accomplished on both Hanniford's building projects and at what stages each of them remained. Whoever took over from her would want those details and both Roger and Killian deserved a full accounting. Furthermore, she owed great gratitude to Roger. To Killian she might not be able to give him what he wanted as a lover or deserved as a wife, but she could and would fulfill her duty as his consultant.

But she was terrified that resigning would totally ruin her. Cut her off from a society that cared for her abilities as a decorator. Financially, she was just beginning to feel comfortable. Able to buy sufficient coal for her fireplaces. A housekeeper in London. A decent, if not superb, school for Camille. When she left Roger and Killian, she would have a time of it applying to other architects. She valued only three here in London. Three. How would she go on if she had to return to counting her pennies for bread? Or worse, living in an East End house where David had found her abiding in one suffocating room?

She locked her front door and raced down the front steps, her trim bonnet in her hand. Rushing to the end of the street, she hailed a hackney cab.

"South Moulton Street," she told the driver and climbed up into the tawdry little black carriage. *Do this*, she told herself *Be free*.

But she wouldn't be. Not of her fears. Or of her desires for this man, this extraordinary man, whom she must give up. For her own serenity. And for his. What did he think of her now that he understood she'd known full well who he was and had not been woman enough to tell him?

He prized honesty. Strength.

She offered him neither. She would be honest enough with herself to admit her failure and strong enough to leave his circle for both their sakes.

She was doing the right thing to resign.

She willed herself to serenity. But her pulse was rapid and her head spun. The past two nights, she'd not slept. She'd looked at herself this morning in her dressing room mirror and gasped. She was ghostly, wan, as if she'd stood in the middle of Piccadilly and let the omnibuses run over her. Earlier this morning, she'd applied powder to her face to cover her splotches from crying and a bit of rouge to her cheeks to give her some color. She'd washed her hair, brushed the wavy mass out as straight as possible in the sunny back courtyard of her house and wound it up into the most elaborate chignon she could manage. She might look like one on death's door, but she'd put the best face possible on her masquerade. She'd lie. She'd live. She'd survive.

If she would also pine, well, that would end. It had to.

Camille was soon to visit for three weeks during her August holiday. Liv had to be ready for her. Though she wondered if that meant she'd stopped thinking of Killian and grieving over his loss.

"Good afternoon, Mister Rush. How are you today?" she greeted Roger Antram's assistant.

"Very well, my lady. Will you have a chair and tea?"

"Tea, yes, thank you." She removed her gloves, the little office stuffy in the July heat. Where was her fan? Ugh. She'd forgotten it at home. Not a surprise. She'd left the house to hail her cab and had to return inside to get her hat. She still hadn't put it on. In addition to losing her client...and her lover, she was also losing her mind.

She stifled a moan and swept aside her skirts to sit. Putting her little reticule and toque hat down on the table, she tapped her toes on the wooden floor. "Is there a delay, Mister Rush?"

"Yes, madam. Actually, no. I was given instructions to have you wait until Mr. Antram was ready for you."

"I see." *What did that mean? Was Killian in there?* "Does Mr. Antram have another appointment?"

"He does, madam."

Who?

The office door opened and Roger himself appeared in the portal. "Come in, Lady Savage."

He seemed wooden, as if he'd smile and all his innards would pop out. And he hadn't addressed her as Lady Savage since before David had died.

She stood. *Feeding myself to the lions.*

Inside, three men she did not know rose to their feet and smiled at her with polite expressions.

Roger made the introductions.

The three were the directors of a private trust established by a man who had died nineteen years previously.

"These gentlemen," Roger told her when the introductions were finished and all five of them sat around his desk, "are the representatives of the board of directors of the Lockern Foundation. They're hiring us to complete a building project established by the last will of Mr. Maxwell Lockern and awarding the contract to us, Lady Savage."

Us. Us. Tension flowed from her like a river. She would prosper. Have a client. Even if she did not work for the Hanniford projects. "How wonderful."

"Forty townhouses with mews, and accompanying houses for tradesmen."

"Forty, you say." A huge project. "A veritable village. How exciting."

"They come to us because they understand you and I know the terrain, the city and the construction crews quite well."

"I see." She smiled and had to ask, "And the location?"

"Brighton. Of course."

"Of course." Her heart thudded in joy and fear.

"We've been impressed with your work for Mr. Killian Hanniford," said the chairman of the directors of the foundation, Mister Winston Taylor. "His townhouses are well on their way. We've seen them. Like the builder. Appreciate the plumbing and the electrical. Very forward of you both to include them. Like the floor plans. Flowing, logical, useful. But we've also toured the foundations of Mister Hanniford's country house. Viewed the plans here. Mr. Antram was kind enough to show them to us. So we know our project will be in good hands."

She inclined her head. Graciousness was necessary. But her hopes of escaping proximity to Brighton died.

"The company," Roger told her, "was formed in 1856. The previous chairman did not find a suitable architect or designer and after he passed away last winter, Mr. Taylor took up the search once more."

"We read about Mr. Hanniford's townhouses and his estate house in *The Brighton Gazette*," said Taylor.

Roger grinned at her. "Mr. Hanniford met with the entire board a few weeks ago."

"That he did," said Taylor. "And we were quite satisfied with his summary of the work you've done for him."

She did not know whether she should clap her hands or cry bitter tears. "Mr. Hanniford recommended you to us?"

"He did indeed, ma'am."

And why wouldn't he? He loved everything Roger and she had done for his projects. To date.

"Very kind of him," said Roger. "Very kind."

More than an hour later, after the three directors had departed to catch the afternoon train back to Brighton from Victoria Station, Liv sat dumfounded in her chair. She had to ask Roger about this marvelous offer. "Have you spoken with Mr. Hanniford about this?"

"Not yet. I thought you two were in Paris." No sign of dismay crossed his brow. He either didn't know or didn't care that Liv and Killian had become more than client and decorator. "Has he returned with you?"

"I don't know. I didn't ask his plans."

"He'll be very pleased that this project came to us because of his work."

"He will."

"And the recommendation will serve as a calling card to even more clients." He crossed his arms and sat, rocking back and forth, happy as a pigeon on a quiet street corner. "We must thank him for his trust in us."

"We must." She could not possibly resign now. If she did, she'd ruin Roger's hopes of this project and other new commissions. She grinned at her professional prospects. She burst with optimism. Those who would define her by her past, scoff at her for her parents' choices, did not know her. Why should she consider their views of her more valid than her own?

She could face Killian. She wanted it. For her own self-respect. Peace of mind. She take with her an apology.

She wanted that for him, for herself, for a daring future she might still grasp with him.

Her mind turned to clothes. She startled at the silliness of her bent of mind. What would she wear to tell him how sorry she was? She could not dress up her failures. Wouldn't try.

She snorted. Ashes and sackcloth would be best. Black would imply she was in mourning. But she wasn't. She was instead...free. So perhaps it was fitting for her to wear nothing. She'd certainly go to him naked. *Naked, in all ways, Liv.*

"You are happy, aren't you, Liv?" Roger intruded on her mental wanderings.

She blinked. "I'm sorry. What did you say, Roger?"

The dark clouds in his expression lifted. "We're on our way to a superb reputation, Liv. I hope you know that."

She smiled at him, her hope and fear quivering like newborn chicks inside her. "Indeed I do."

❦

Pierce stood with him to bid the last of their guests good night. The dinner party had included a gilded array of French industrialists as well as the banker Rothschild, a Belgian pharmaceutical company owner and a Swiss maker of precision clocks and watches. Remy, Marianne and the Princess d'Aumale were the only other family guests, but they were the perfect complements to the gathering. Remy's mother knew each person and perhaps even their pedigree by heart. Remy knew them because many had commissioned sculptures from him. And Marianne brought her love of painting to the group, especially her descriptions of how popular renderings of women and children were becoming among artists and patrons. The evening lacked only one thing.

Liv. Whom he'd hoped would've played Chopin for them.

Liv. Who would've been his hostess. For the first time.

Liv. Who would've worn his ring as his fiancée.

"A wonderful evening, Killian," Princess d'Aumale said as he kissed both her cheeks. "*Merci beaucoup.* I will take my carriage. Valmont is here at the door, I think. *Oui*," she said as she peered through the open portal. "Marianne told me you wish to speak to her and Remy. I will go ahead. My grandson needs his Nana to kiss him, you see, before he goes to sleep."

Killian chuckled as he thanked her. "Yes, I will send them home in my own carriage, *Madame. Merci beaucoup* for your company tonight."

"*Mon cher*, I will readily appear for fine champagne, superb cuisine and your family's wit." She considered Pierce who stood next to Killian. "This young man is a charmer. A wonder you are not married yet, Pierce."

His son blushed. "*Madame*, I am afraid I choose the wrong women."

Killian found it difficult to smile. Pierce concentrated on one woman, one wrong woman, too much. She was married, unavailable to him. *Like Liv is to me.*

Perhaps he and I are both foolish.

"Change that, young man." She tapped her fan to Pierce's white silk cravat. "You are too handsome and much too accomplished to waste it on a woman who cannot love you as you deserve."

Pierce knew how to cover his distress with a dashing grin. "*Merci, Madame.* I shall take your advice."

"Do. *Au revoir!*"

"Good Christ," Pierce whispered as the lady swept through their front entrance. "Do I wear my care for Elanna like a sign?"

Lily had reported in a recent letter that Elanna had recently left her home in the country to take up residence in the Carbury townhouse in London. She had not taken her newborn son with her, but left him to the nurses. Her husband, the earl, had arrived at Willowreach, his wife's farewell note crushed in his hand, to berate Julian for encouraging her.

"'Julian vehemently denied any such thing. We had quite a scene here,'" Lily wrote. "'I was concerned Carbury had been drinking and he and Julian would come to blows. As it was, Julian had two footmen show the man the door and warned him never to return again with such accusations.'"

"Perhaps you need to examine what it is you are doing, Pierce."

He scowled. "I care for her. She's so unhappy, Father."

"What has she ever brought you, son?"

Shaking his head, Pierce had no answer.

"If she appeals to your tender heart, is it because she chooses to portray herself as the tragic victim?" His question touched a chord in him. *Liv refuses to be a victim. Rejects pity. And has risen above her circumstances. Until now. With me.*

"Oh, I wish I knew the answer, Father." He shoved his hands in his tuxedo trouser pockets. "I keep asking myself why I compare all females to her when I could have my choice of any young woman with no problems, no husband, no baby."

"When you know the answer, you'll move on."

He inhaled. "And in the meantime, I'm for bed. Great dinner party. Please say goodnight to Marianne and Remy for me, will you?"

"I will." He watched his son climb the stairs and turned for the salon.

Marianne sat beside her husband on a settee, laughing with him as he sipped a brandy.

He grinned at them. "I'm delighted to see that happiness continues after the birth of your first child."

"How could it not?" Remy said to him, curling an arm around his wife's shoulders. "I have the finest woman in the world to myself."

Killian nodded and went to the corner where the butler had set out the brandy decanter and cigars on the serving cart. He asked if Remy would care for another pour, but the man refused politely. Pouring himself a good measure of spirits, Killian strode over to face them and take a seat in the grand Rococo upholstered chair. He downed a drink, looking for the right words to broach his subject.

Marianne grew grave.

Her husband took another sip.

"Liv returned to London yesterday."

They waited, patient and placid. He'd told them that when they arrived and they'd expressed their disappointment.

"At the restaurant, the man who accompanied Edouard Montand was once a friend of her husband. His presence disturbed her and I have a small understanding of the cause."

Remy cleared his throat and got to his feet. "May I?" he gestured to the cart.

"Of course."

Marianne sat with concern wrinkling her brow. Killian doubted she knew much of Liv's past and so he waited until Remy was ready to tell him more.

"Liv's mother was a second cousin to my own," he said when he returned and took his place beside his wife. "The woman was, as some term it in England, nervous. She was from the English aristocracy, a younger daughter with only a small widow's portion and no particular talents or graces to commend her. Their marriage was not notable for its happiness. Liv was their only child. Her father was a viscount of little means and a small estate. He owned stock in a few companies, but he was not skilled at administration."

Remy studied his glass, seeming reluctant to go on. "At a young age, he negotiated away his shares in his greatest holding. As a result, the family could not live as they had. The debts were double their income and the tenants suffered. I understand many simply left for London and the land went untilled. Liv's mother refused to go out into society. On a few occasions, they found her in the streets in her nightrail, muttering obscenities. She was, they say, prone to hurting herself. Mama sent funds each month to help them. I think for years they lived off that. Liv became her parents' caretaker. Cook, maid, who knows what else. After a few years when her mother became unmanageable, Liv sent her mother to a secluded home in the country. She and her father moved to a smaller house east of London near the docks, and soon after her father hung himself."

"A very sad life," Killian said. Shock did not roll through him. As soon as she'd told him her maiden name, he'd recoiled. All the horror of his greatest disaster rained upon him like acid. "For all of them."

"A scandal Liv wished to escape."

Killian felt the despair of all Liv had lived through. She'd been the only one to stand up through financial decline, madness and suicide. "And when did she marry?"

"A few weeks after she buried her father, David visited her. From what I understand from bits and pieces of Liv's conversations when she'd visit Mama and me, his family and Liv's had known each other forever. She and David grew up as neighbors until her father's loss of his businesses. David was aware of Liv's circumstances. He visited often and was appalled at their circumstances. He might even have given Liv money to aid them."

"Why didn't he marry her before the death of her father?"

Remy inhaled. "He didn't have to. But about the same time that Liv's father died, David had his own challenges. He'd long been known as a dandy. A fine dresser, owing much more to his tailor than appropriate for a man of his limited means. He had fine tastes in Spitalfields silks and Aubusson carpets, Japanese lacquers. But he also showed certain, shall we say, proclivities toward other men and that is not tolerated well in English society."

Killian was more interested in her husband's temperament. "He was a kind man?"

"Gentle, soft-spoken, intelligent. But he was growing careless with his assignations and he'd had a few occasions when in London, that he'd been discovered with men of a different repute."

Killian stared at Remy who honored Liv's husband with polite words. "He was a homosexual."

Remy nodded. "He was. Here in France we look the other way. Allow people their rightful choice of lovers. But in

England, they cannot overlook public displays of affections such as that. Their moral code demands conformity."

"With a vengeance." Killian had had experience with the English demand for a patina of respectability. His oldest daughter Lily had married partly because she was discovered with her future husband in questionable circumstances. Fortunately she and her husband Julian adored each other so the wedding had been a joyous occasion and the hint of impropriety had not destroyed them. His youngest daughter Ada had escaped similar censure when she'd had a romp in Cherbourg last summer with her friends. The current scandal that brewed within his extended family was a virulent one of the marital strife between Julian's sister Elanna and her husband, the earl of Carbury.

"People are not kind," Marianne said with a watery smile at Killian.

She had also escaped censure when she'd lived with Remy up in Montmartre for a month last year. Remy had warned his friends to breathe not a word of her presence in his house. His fellow artists, respectful and careful of each other, had complied.

Killian's whole family had felt the lick of gossip's destructive flames. But he himself was the greatest villain. During the war, he'd sailed his three ships through the Yankee blockade to Manchester and Portsmouth. Carrying cotton from the Confederates, he brought home gunpowder and rifles. He'd traded for profit. He'd prolonged the fighting and he had become ashamed of it. Yes, the proceeds had made him a rich man. A feared man. A man who reformed because his wife despised his actions—and prodded his conscience.

"Who are you, Killian?" she'd asked him one morning, unsympathetic and angry after the unnecessary loss of a ship and eight of his seamen in a hurricane off the Chesapeake Bay. "A poor man who'd risk the lives of good men to earn a dollar? A man who'd fuel the fires of war to gain a fortune? A man who earns his daily bread by cheating others out of theirs? Or a man who offers others a way up and out of poverty? Decide. Do it quickly because I'd like once more to be proud of you."

Months later, he refitted his two remaining ships. Ended the illegal English trade. Formed an alliance—and avoided prosecution as a traitor to the Union to transport supplies to rebuild railroads in the southern states. His wife smiled at him once again. He smiled at himself. For a few months. Until that other disaster in England had reached his ears. That other disaster that paralyzed him with shame. And guilt. If he would not trade guns to prolong an ugly war, would he countenance a purchase that was illegally negotiated...and killed a man?

He'd walked through the fires of hell years ago to deal with that. And still today he'd had no closure on the news.

Now he was in love with the woman who had been burned by that same fire. Because he'd set her family ablaze, she had suffered. Yet, through it all, she had cared for her parents and endured hardship and loss. She'd been brave.

He loved her more. Much more than he had known. He was proud of her. His challenge was not simply to tell her, but to prove it to her. But how?

"Liv's marriage?" He had to learn if she'd gained some peace in it. "Was it happy?"

"I believe in some ways, yes," Remy said. "David needed to marry a woman of good moral reputation. She needed to be lifted out of the mire of her existence. They had a pact. The two of them came to Paris for their wedding trip. I was young. What? Twenty? Twenty-one? They came to dinner with Mama and me one night and we did enjoy ourselves. Liv seemed relieved to be married."

"I think she was," Killian said with conviction.

"David appeared happy, too. Why wouldn't he be? He had legitimacy. He was safe. When they left I recall Mama and I agreed that they might make a good union of it. They must have come to an understanding because later Camille was born."

"They became decorators," Killian said.

"*Oui*, partners. David had been trying his hand at it and Liv learned from him. When they began to work with one certain architect, they did very well."

"Roger Antram. He designs my country house and my townhouses in Brighton. A good man. Ethical. I like him tremendously."

"David and Liv did well with him. They earned a living and gained a solid reputation that overlooked her past and his."

"And when David died, what happened?"

"Liv was aggrieved. She loved him as a friend, the man who saved her from disgrace and despair. When I received Liv's telegram that he'd died, I attended the funeral. The least I could do, I thought. Yesterday, I told Marianne that I believed that gentleman with Edouard in the Place du Tertre the other day looked familiar. I do believe he was there."

"He was."

They sat for a long minute, regarding each other.

"There is more, isn't there, Remy?"

"I left out much."

Killian gripped his glass. He needed two more facts before he could attempt once more to rectify this injustice. "What year was her father bankrupted?"

Remy stared at him. Sorrow lined his features. "Killian, you torture yourself. Is this necessary?"

"It is. I must verify everything before I go to my solicitor in the City and to the police. So tell me, Remy, if you know when Liv's father suffered his financial blow."

"Sixty-one. Sixty-two?"

"During our American civil war."

"*Oui.* He owned a shipping company that declined from lack of cotton imports when the Federals blockaded shipments to England. He had to sell."

"Do you know the English port?"

Remy stared at him with sad eyes. "I do."

The coincidence is a hellish irony. The perfect reason for Liv to hate me. "Liverpool."

Remy nodded once, then drained his glass and took the hand of his wife to help her up. "Come along, *ma chèrie.* We must leave your uncle to his memories."

CHAPTER 17

August, 1879
Brighton

Liv climbed the hill to the construction site, Camille close behind her. As it was a brilliant Saturday morning, Liv had promised her daughter a day on the promenade. Ices in a cup, fresh steamed shrimp from a monger's stall, perhaps even a sail on the boat in the city regatta that set out each afternoon for a short sail along the shore.

Camille was eager to get out of Liv's tiny rented townhouse. For the past week, she'd been cooped up there because of rain or dreary cold mist. At last at dawn, sun had broken through the clouds and Liv was eager to show her daughter a happy day and to check on progress on Killian's house.

Liv shaded her eyes with a hand to the straw brim of her hat, smiling at the two men on the scaffolding. "Hello, there!"

"Hallo, milady!" One of the carpenters waved to her from atop his ladder leaning against the framework for the roof. "Hot to be out today!"

"It is. But we've come for the sunshine!"

"Oh, Mama. It's magnificent."

Liv turned to Camille who had a hand to her heart, her mouth agog as she gazed up at the expanse that was to be the grand county home of the American millionaire, Killian Hanniford.

The Manor gave the appearance of sitting into the eyebrow of the hill. The curving drive added grace to the approach. The friendliness and open terrain added a charm that shimmered in the white stone, delineated by pale bricks in herringbone at hip height. The chimneys for the many fireplaces dotted the roof at regular points and gave punctuation to the Palladian order of the serene front and each side.

Inside, she had ordered Italian marble tiles for the rotunda foyer and for the grand staircase. The entry was a peaceful circle that opened so that one room led grandly to another. Each room was of a dimension that could accommodate twenty in conversational groups. The dining room could hold thirty. The breakfast room held ten. The drawing room looked out over the west lawn and in the large nook in the floor were colored tiles laid into a design of the map of the world. All floors were fireproofed, double-framed with concrete and iron. The kitchen, in so many houses situated far from the dining areas, in this house was a few steps away. Food would be delivered hot and fragrant to the owners.

A pleasant benefit for the staff, a nearby kitchen meant footmen need not run from yards away to serve course after course—and deliver them still warm as cook intended. Those employed at the house could count other advantages. The servants quarters on the third floor were a full height, not the three-quarters of many manors, which meant they could stand upright in their own rooms. Even the kitchen quarters downstairs for cook and her maids was extraordinary in size. What the owners and family of this house would have in size and care would be shared in many ways by those who waited upon them. Even the carriage house, the stables and the kitchen garden and stillroom were dry, cool, heated with a fire place and also well ventilated.

The modern amenities that Killian had demanded tried the expertise of the masons and the plumbers. But they improvised and they learned new techniques. They used new techniques to secure flanges on the elbow joints and experimented with copper for the drainage and the septic systems. If at first they laughed over Hanniford's requirements, now as they implemented new safety for the electrical wiring and bigger water tanks for the w.c.s, they were very happy they did. What they learned here, they could use elsewhere. They talked over their pail lunches of how they'd gain fame and fortune in the long run.

But all of her time here had not been totally focused on the house.

These past three weeks had allowed Liv breathing room to consider her actions. She was not proud of herself. She'd been less than honest with Killian about her rejection of him. And the ache in her heart reminded her with every step she took that she missed him. And she loved him.

That revelation burst upon her the day after her meeting with Roger. She recalled Killian's laughter, his kindness, his joy in his family and his charming pursuit of her favor. For herself and him and what they might share, she buried her old fear of others, their critiques, their cruelty. Had any one of the lofty One Hundred aided her? Other than David who had married her, and Remy and his mother who had sent her family funds, who among those whose favor she had honored, had been kind and helpful to her? Who among them had smiled upon her in her poverty or in her travail to keep her parents clothed and fed? Who had treasured her?

None.

To whom did she owe her loyalty? Her respect? Her devotion?

David was dead. Remy and his mother were alive. They were as thrilled to see her as in the days when she was an innocent girl visiting with her mama—and she treasured them.

Aside from that, she had saved herself from despair and poverty. She had married David, not for romantic love, but she had been not only loyal but also honest to him and herself about her motives.

She could now free herself of her fear of society to accept the possibility of happiness with a man who had in his own way changed for the better. A man who had decided—soon after the horrid negotiation with her father for his company —to be a better man?

If she could find her way back into his good graces, she hoped to ameliorate the sins of her past, just as he had his. In that vein, she had worked diligently on this house. This edifice which would stand as a haven for the Hannifords she hoped might also serve as a window to how people might resolve to build new futures for themselves.

She had written to him. In a note separate from her usual updates on the buildings' progress, she asked to see him soon. She was polite, informal. She offered to go up to London if that was convenient for him. Or she'd welcome him to her home in Brighton. She did not say that if he did not wish to see her, she would understand. Whatever his view of her since Paris, she must offer him her apology in person. It was the only way to go on with her life with any integirty.

He had replied the next day. "'I have a pressing matter I must investigate. After that, I will come to Brighton to meet with you.'"

Disappointed that she had no definite date from him, she

noted his polite tone...and his agreement to meet her. She had to accept that. In the meantime to occupy her, she had her work...and her daughter.

"Can we go inside?" Camille's jade green gaze danced over the rafters, down along the alabaster columns. "I need to see it. I shall use it in my next novel."

Liv laughed. "I thought you liked gloomy castles with spider webs dripping from the curtain walls."

Camille stuck out her tongue. "I'm tired of brooding heroes. I'm up for a romp of the Regency period."

"Dear heavens." Liv put a hand to her heart like an over-dramatic actress. "A duke?"

"Or a rogue who's a second son. His papa likes his oldest boy. Sedate and prudent."

"Boring."

"True. We need a man who rouses the spirit, breaks a few rules and then repents."

Liv nodded. "More exciting."

"There you are! So this house with its creamy stone and meandering front drive is just the setting for the return of the prodigal son."

Liv laughed and put an arm around her girl's shoulders. Camille, with her sixteenth birthday next week, was as tall as Liv now. She was an elegant swan, with perfect pink cheeks and small white teeth, a river of golden hair streaked with glistening copper. She was quite breath-taking to look at. In fact, when they'd dined out these past few evenings, Liv had noticed the covetous glances sent to her gorgeous daughter. If she wished it, Camille could marry early and quite well. But Liv hoped she'd wait a very long time to choose a groom. If she could persuade her daughter to enjoy that opportunity, then Liv predicted her only child would find the perfect man to love and to love her in return.

Liv took the rocky path toward the front steps.

"I hear the sea."

Liv looked back at Camille who had paused, her eyes closed, a rapturous look on her face.

She spun and headed for the cliff. "I have to see it! Come on, Mama!"

"Wait for me!" Liv ran behind her daughter.

Camille came to an abrupt halt in front of the Dominican abbey's arches. Wild flowers growing around her feet, they decorated her skirt as if they'd been painted there. A glorious riot of summertime blooms, pinks, yellows and whites dotted her daughter's pale green muslin gown. She trailed her fingertips through the blossoms, scattering petals in the breeze. "Oh, this is glorious. I bet it's wonderful on a moonlit night. A marvelous place to be kissed and to fall in love."

Camille's words had Liv wrapping her arms around her waist, envisioning what it must be like to be romanced in such a place. *I could hope for that. Want it badly. Once in my life.* "Enchanting, yes. It is."

Camille shot her a wild look. "You'll leave it just like this, won't you? Mr. Hanniford won't make you cut down the flowers and put up giant rhododendrons and prickly roses, I hope."

"I doubt it. He likes this as it is. Although we will clear the path here from the house and build a secure terrace to have easy access to the arches."

"Superb! So it will be easy to waltz out here too. An orchestra inside in the—" She pointed toward the walled stones of the house. "What will that be? That room that fronts this view?"

"An orangerie with large French doors."

"So you could dance in there?"

"I suppose so, yes." She turned to the opening where the

doors would go and she could see inside, Killian in an elegant swallowtail welcoming his guests and dancing with...me.

"The winds won't blow out the glass?" Camille asked, her knowledge of building and decor sound at her age.

"No. They will be double paned. Unusual but necessary. Sturdy to counter the seaward winds, but light enough to allow the brilliance of the view inside."

"Like a conservatory for the sea and the sun and the wild flowers of Sussex."

Liv laughed. "Come inside, my girl. You are waxing poetic."

"I must have venues, you know. Wonderful places for assignations."

Liv arched a brow at her. "Keep those venues in your imagination, my dear. Not in your experience for many years to come."

"I shall fall in love in an instant, Mama." Camille said it as if it were ordained. "You've always known it."

"Dear god. I do hope not. Rogues abound. I do hope you have the sense to wait to fall for a man who can complement you in energy as well as imagination."

Camille picked up her skirt and swished the fabric like a coquette. "He, whoever he is, must not be boring."

"Trust me. He won't be if he must keep up with you." She looped her arm through her daughter's. "Let's see the house."

Camille adored every inch of the place. She'd oo-ed and ahh-ed in the drawing room, sighed in the long gallery, pretended to play an imaginary piano in the small salon, twirled about in the orangerie like a debutante before she stood in awe in the massive kitchen. "Dear me, Mama! Who are we feeding in this cavern?"

"A large family will visit here, never forget. And there's room for all of them. They must be fed well."

"Oh, yes. I'd forgotten all of them who'd been to Remy's

wedding." She trailed her hand along the wooden frame where the roasting fireplace would stand. "Two daughters, one unmarried, and one married to the Duke of Seton. They have one son."

"Remy's new wife is Mr. Hanniford's niece."

"And they have their son. Bertrand, is it?"

Liv nodded. "Rand, they call him."

"And Mr. Hanniford has a son. Did I meet him at Remy's wedding?"

"You did," declared a rich bass voice.

Liv whirled around to see Pierce Hanniford grinning at her.

"Hello, Liv!" Pierce picked his way over piles of wooden wainscoting to take Liv by the shoulders and kiss her on both cheeks. "How are you?"

"I'm well," she said as she looked straight ahead into the silver fires of Killian's searching gaze.

"Camille, how wonderful." Pierce moved toward her daughter and left Liv facing the man she'd yearned to see again.

"Hello, Liv," Killian greeted her quietly. "How are you?"

"Well," she told him and then summoned the pluck for more of the truth. "Now that I see you, I am much better."

That transformed his impersonal gaze into a benevolent smile. "I'm very glad to hear it."

She wanted to abduct him, blurt out all her new resolutions. But his reticence and the fact that he'd brought Pierce with him, signaled now was not the best time. At a loss how to proceed, she tried for the mundane. "You're here for the day?"

"We took the nine-thirty excursion train from Victoria. Lucky we got a seat!"

"It's always crowded on Saturday."

"Half of London," said Pierce, "had climbed aboard."

Liv found her voice and her hope. "Today the weather means it is a wonderful day to be in Brighton."

"I remember," he said and his words mingled with the memory so that she fought tears in her eyes.

He fished a handkerchief from his waistcoat pocket and tucked it in her hand. "Don't cry, Liv. Everything will be fine."

She dabbed at her lashes. The lump in her throat was big as a boulder. "I want to tell you how sorry I am. For the argument. For everything. I've so much to explain."

"I'm glad to hear that. We need time to heal old wounds. Let's take it, shall we?"

This was the Killian she loved, the kind and gentle man. She beamed at him. "By all means. I'd like to walk you through the house."

"My dear, I saw the receipts yesterday at Roger's. You're spending me out of existence with your choices," he said on a chuckle, "so you'd better make this a grand tour."

"Oh!" She clutched the handkerchief to her chest, her brain suddenly mush. She was so overjoyed to see him. Handsome charming debonair Killian. "I've spent too much? But—but Roger said you told him I had the run of it. Up to—um—how much? I—I can't recall."

"Forty thousand pounds. Yes, I did say that."

"But now it's too much? Well, well. All right. All right." She put one hand to her chest, one to her temple. "I can cut back."

He grabbed her hand, the one against her chest and she could wager he felt how frantically her heart beat. "Don't you dare."

"No? I don't understand. If you want me to stop spending then I—"

"I was teasing you. I want you to have whatever you want, Liv. I don't care how much it costs."

She tipped her head. "I'm confused. What are you saying?"

He tucked her arm in his and patted her hand. "Just show me the house, Liv. Tell me how wonderful it will be to live here."

⚜

"Shall we go outside and start in?" she asked, her mind more calm, her words more practical when talking about architecture and design.

"Let's. We'll leave Pierce here to entertain Camille."

Liv glanced at the couple and shook her head. "I would say it seems the other way round."

"She is a delightful girl. I remember meeting her at Marianne and Remy's wedding."

"Thank you. I find her...effervescent. She fills me with pride. Her vivacity for life."

"I can see Pierce finds her amusing."

Killian's son and her daughter were laughing together.

"Camille will be coming out soon," he said.

"No. She'll turn sixteen in a week, but she won't have a debut." Liv rolled a shoulder, sensitive about this issue. "I cannot afford it. She doesn't expect it. Doesn't want it."

"I understand," he said. "Lily was married before she could have one, but she didn't want it anyway. Marianne was a widow and couldn't bear the idea of it in any case. And Ada flatly refuses. She finds it just as much fun to drive the men of the town crazy without adding the tensions of being presented at court."

"Wise of them. Camille says she'll learn more if she remains an observer of society rather than a participant."

"Oh, what does she observe?" he asked with a grin.

"She's a writer. Or an aspiring one."

"Bravo," he said as they made their way across the uncut lawn to the entrance of the house. "A poet, I would imagine."

"Mmm. She is dreamy. But no. Though she tells me she'll change, she puts her pen to gothic romances. Gloomy men in towers. Virginal young ladies in dire circumstances. They pine for each other. "

He had a wicked half smile to his lips. "Have you read her work?"

"I have. She's quite eloquent. One wonders how and when children learn what they do. She didn't decide to read anything until she was ten and then she read everything, even the labels on tins and store flyers. Most of it aloud, too. A few months ago, she told me she sent off one of her stories to a publisher in London."

He chuckled. "Any word yet?"

"Nothing. I don't expect any."

"Don't be too sure. Pierce made his first fortune at eighteen investing in a copper mining company in Colorado. No one else thought it had a chance. He did." He came to a stop before the porch at the entrance to the house and waved a hand above him. "The coach entrance?"

"Exactly. Larger than usual by a third to accommodate two traveling coaches pulling to the front door at the same time."

"Have you decided on the columns?"

"Doric. Simple. Orderly."

He swung around to view the green before them. "I like the escalation of the land. A plane. A welcoming court. And the drive curves around the main block to the carriage house and stables."

"And to the kitchen garden. I think your cook, whoever she is, will love the expanse. The entire plan for the landscape takes advantage of the serenity of the view."

"I liked the plan when Roger first showed it to me. I

didn't want a castle on a hill, but a home nestled in its proper place."

She stared at him. He was not a king defending his realm by force. But a king of commerce with enough humility to display it in his style of a new home. "Did you hire Roger because of his reputation?"

He narrowed those piercing silver eyes at her. "I did. Not because you worked for him, Liv. If that's what you're really asking me. I had asked among my friends and acquaintances for recommendations for architects. I'm not in the habit of hiring people unless I'm impressed with their potential. And though I knew you worked with Roger, I planned to see you again whether or not you worked on my projects."

"Thank you. I had to ask."

"I understand."

"Shall we go in?"

"We should," she said, her hope to resolve their conflict growing more positive by the minute.

Stepping through the hollow of what would become the double doors into the foyer, they stood on the Italian cream and honeyed marble parquet tiles.

"As you can see if you stand here," she said and took his hand to lead him nearer to her, "you turn right to climb the grand staircase. Or if you wish to turn left you have a straight line of sight from the entrance through to the long gallery and large French doors leading to the outside terrace and the Dominican arches. Your view of the sea will be unobstructed. On a clear day, this will be a sweep to the sun and the water. With the doors open, I predict you'll hear the waves upon the shore."

She stood entranced by the prospect.

When she tore her attention to him, he was smiling down at her. "You hear them now?"

She nodded. "Even though it's not high tide? I do."

"Show me the rest." He offered his arm again.

This time when she took it, she felt a rush of joy. He was here. He'd come to be with her, enjoy her company and he was not angry. He was not demanding explanations, but had come, she was certain now, to see if there was hope they might find a way forward into a future. At least as friends.

And if I am fortunate, perhaps more.

CHAPTER 18

"**S**plendid dinner," Killian told Liv two Saturdays later as the four sat in Liv's small dining room in her rented townhouse on the Marine Parade. "You are an excellent cook."

Killian would be discreet to say nothing of his previous visit here. Camille should not hear of her mother's brief affair, and Pierce gave no hints of it.

"It takes a delicate hand not to over-bake the fish," said Camille. "Mama is very quick to sauté them just right."

"And the cream cake is one I could have again," said Pierce with a grin.

"You could have another piece," Liv said.

"No, I could not!" Pierce said with a pat to his stomach.

"But now, it's time we washed the dishes," Killian said. "We don't want to miss the band."

Camille clasped her hands together. "The 16th Lancers. They're playing only from eight o'clock to ten."

Killian said, "Precisely. What do you say, Pierce?"

"But—" Liv objected. "My maid is here to do this."

"We created more work for her than she normally has,"

Killian said. "So, no. We'll help! No excuses. I said we've come to take you dancing on the promenade tonight and we will!"

Camille beamed at them. "Me, too, I hope."

Pierce feigned horror. "How could we possibly take a child like you?"

"Oh!" she squinted at him. "You don't think I can dance."

"Have they taught you to waltz at that school you go to?"

"I'll show you a step or two, you presumptuous man. Besides," Camille said and folded her arms, "if you don't take me along, I shall sneak out and find you. A total scandal. Then what will you do?"

Pierce spread his hand wide. "Haul you over my shoulder and bring you home."

"Mama," Camille pleaded, her lovely face an utter wreck. "Tell them I can come."

Liv grinned at her daughter. "I wouldn't dream of leaving you here."

"All right! That's settled," Killian said as he shoved back his chair. "Dishes! Now!"

For three Saturdays, he and Pierce had taken the early train down to Brighton. He'd asked his son to come along with him, intent on making the visits light-hearted affairs. Nonetheless, Liv had attempted to apologize in depth for her behavior, but he'd blocked her.

"I have my own explanations to offer, but I am not yet ready," he'd declared.

"Why?" She frowned, insisting he tell her.

"I owe you as much—perhaps more—than you may think you owe me. I should have news soon. Until then, we'll enjoy ourselves. Rekindle our friendship and our affections." He'd offered her a consoling smile. "Soon, my darling. Soon."

He'd broached no subjects other than the polite ones or those that pertained to the construction of his country house or his townhouses. Occasionally, he and Liv discussed the other project she supervised, that of the Lockern Foundation and their forty townhouses.

"I'm pleased with that commission," she'd told him earlier today. "I owe you my thanks for that recommendation."

"You earned that on merit. I would not have given any praise, if you **and Roger** didn't deserve it."

"I'm pleased at that, too," she said and squeezed his hand.

That and the easy way she looped her arm through his as they strolled along his landscape or the small city of Brighton were the only physical expressions of her growing ease with him. She didn't cast about when they were out along the Parade or in a restaurant. For whatever reasons, she was at ease with him. What Remy had told him of her youth and family had given him enough clues to the reasons she'd not wished to associate with him. He only hoped time and his love for her might salve the wound. Love could cure much, but not every wrong doing. He was old enough and wise enough to acknowledge the pain of that. But he had to try to bring her to him. If he had to wait years, he would.

This renewal of their friendship he hoped would be gradual, a mutual acceptance of what was inevitable. He loved her. And though she had not declared it, Killian could see in her words, her smiles that she cared for him. Although she had to come to the statement of it in her own good time, he worried that she could never love him enough to forgive the past and marry him.

Pierce was a fine companion for these trips. Jovial, joking with him, Pierce understood Killian's sorrow that Liv had rejected his proposal. So he was good enough to come along. Though today, he had not been keen to leave London. On the train, he'd confided that he'd called upon Elanna yesterday in her London townhouse.

"She's horribly unhappy," Pierce had told him. "No one

receives her by herself. She's furious at the snub. Carbury's been up to London just this week again to barge in and demand she return home."

"It is his house and his wife," Killian said with foreboding in his heart. His intelligent son was obsessed with the young and foolish Countess of Carbury and could not stop himself from interfering. "And you can and should do nothing to irritate the situation."

"I know. I do know. She's like...a drug. I cannot stop. Nor can Phillip Leland. He was leaving as I arrived."

"Leland's constant attentions make matters worse. Carbury already hates Leland and suspects him of 'criminal conversation'. If he becomes incensed and sues for divorce, he may include any other man he suspects on a list."

"Me?" Pierce turned beat red in fury. "Absurd. He knows I'm her friend."

"Leland probably says the same."

But Carbury was so incensed about his wife's spurning him, he would reject reasonable explanations. He could do anything. Anything at all.

Killian wished he could do more to distract his son from the web of the seductive countess. Warning him of disgrace had not seemed to be sufficient.

At least, Pierce was eager to come along to Brighton each Saturday and help him renew his friendship with Liv. He hadn't expected to fall in love. Not at his age. But he couldn't help the admiration he felt for Liv...or the desire. To learn that she was the daughter of the man whose livelihood he had ruined had shocked him. But it also resurrected in him a belief that on rare occasions in one's life it was possible to correct the harm one had done to another.

Killian prayed his efforts to make amends to Liv would not be in vain—and that she might come to love him and live with him as his wife.

"Shall we go?" Camille asked when they'd dried the last plate. "I'm ready and the band begins at eight o'clock on the stroke."

⚜

"Are you chilled?" Killian asked her as they found a spot on the terrace sheltered from the sea by the bandstand. "The air has turned colder."

"It will rain tomorrow, I think," she said and leaned against the wooden rail that enclosed the public dance floor.

"You can have my coat."

"I don't need it," she said, though she gathered her wool shawl around her throat. Turning aside to watch Camille and Pierce waltzing to the band's rendition of a Viennese tune, she found her voice and her logic. "They're very attuned to each other. Some couples never get the rhythm right."

"We could."

She took that opening to say her peace. Admiring the sharp, clean lines of his handsome face, she said, "We could. What remains is for me to tell you the real reason I refused you that day. Will you let me now?"

His mouth curved at one corner. Reaching out, he smoothed tendrils of her hair from her cheek. It was the most intimately he'd touched her since they'd parted in the Grand Hotel. "Please."

"When I went to Elanna's wedding a year ago June, I went out of curiosity to see you. I had no intention to meet you. None at all. In fact, I wished only to view you from afar. The rich American robber baron who had come to London with his family."

He said nothing, but as his expression darkened into a frown, she saw he waited for the whole of it.

"I hated you."

He grimaced, jerking away as if she'd struck him.

"I was rude to you and although I hadn't intended harsh words, I chastised myself for my childish behavior. Even if you did not know who I was, I'd been brutish to you. So when I received the invitation to attend Marianne's and Remy's wedding in Paris, I had to go. I intended to apologize to you."

"And to tell me who you were?"

She tipped her head, whimsical in her denial. "I had to, didn't I, because I was trapped in my own vise. I was attracted to you. Charmed by your smile when I was so rude to you. You could forgive that? It was astonishing. Against all my intentions, all my instincts, I found you irresistible."

He stared at his shoes. "And?"

"I hated myself for it."

His dark brows shot high. In the rays of the gas lamps, his silver eyes were brilliant with confusion.

Once again, she was ashamed of herself.

"Not the usual way to begin a love affair is it?" he said, glancing at anyone and anything but her.

It was her turn to stare at her shoes. "No. I grew to care for you quickly. Too quickly. My negative feelings for you dissolved like rain in the sun. Those weeks with you in Willowreach—with all your family—showed me who you were. Kind. Vigilant. Honest. I admired you. Cared for you. At first, I told myself it was the fact that I'd been starved for affection for decades. Then I decided my attraction to you was lust. Silly to think a woman of my age could want a man like that. But there you have it. Need, desire and finally delight in your company. The more I saw you, the less I was compelled to dislike you. I was caught in a web of my own design. I hated that. I had to change."

"Good."

She gave him a wan smile. "The time I spent with you at

Willowreach, the enjoyment I saw you have in your family touched me. And I—oh!—I enjoyed it too. I spoke of an idyll, a time apart, and it was that for me. Because you were there, a comfort, a bulwark against fear, even the likes of Carbury. You showed me what a man could be, should be to his family."

He listened, his gaze in hers, without response.

She owed him more. "Your house has been a delight to create. The fact that you gave me rein meant I conjured you up as I saw you. I was down to the man, the real man, though I saw only my interpretation of you. And I like him. In the flesh. In my reverie, too. To imagine you in the small drawing room reading a newspaper or at a desk in the office working has meant I've seen you, not as others have painted you, but as you truly are."

Pain wrinkled his brow. "And how is that?"

"A man who works hard, who is devoted to his family and who has ethics about the businesses he owns."

He leaned an elbow on the rail and turned to look out to sea. "That has not always been so."

"I know."

He took both her hands. "When I was young, I was also very hungry. My sister and I had sailed to America with a pittance she'd earned. Poverty makes you mean. And angry."

"That I understand."

"I won't ingratiate myself with you by telling you a tale of misery. That would not be fair. But I will tell you that when I first earned money, enough of it, to buy other men's businesses, I did so without regard to ethics. I grew wealthy. I also grew ruthless. I stopped only when I learned that a man I'd ruined had hung himself."

She struggled to speak. "My father."

He winced. "Robert Emley, Lord Newton, who owned Emley Shipping Limited sold me his majority stock in eighteen sixty-one. I found an ad in the *Liverpool Daily Post*, went to meet the broker in Water Street. He was a shark, fast talking, rough. But I needed more ships. I needed them soon. I knew how the South would fall to the North. I'd traveled in those ports and saw how meager their defenses and their resources.

"For weeks, I negotiated the asking price of those two steamers for less than they were worth. I knew finances of many British shipping companies were in jeopardy. Our war and problems in trade with China and India wrecked havoc on the economy here. Prices were high and getting more ridiculous every day."

He squinted into the distance, shame and sorrow haunted his magnificent eyes.

"I never met the owner, Emley, but two months later my banker in the City of London paid the broker the first of three installments of the sales figure. I took over the two steamers and hired a crew to supplement the old. We prospered. I used them along the Irish Sea out of Liverpool into Dublin and Waterford. A few months later, my banker informed me that the broker failed to appear to take his last payment. He seemed to have disappeared."

Liv caught her breath. "Do you think the broker cheated my father on the sale?"

"I did learn soon afterward that he never collected the last third." He faced her squarely and in the dark, his face was tortured. "Last month, I launched a new investigation with my banker, my solicitor and Scotland Yard. We must find this man and put him in jail."

Killian had gone to the police as well as his banker and solicitor. Her heart swelled with gratitude. "Oh, Killian. How can I ever thank you for that?"

"If we find him, I might allow it. But, Liv, I am to blame here."

She could have been polite and objected, but he was right.

"So you see, if your father was paid the right amounts of the first two installments is a matter we must try to discover. If you have any records, that would help."

Astonished, she cleared her head. "I may have the papers, yes."

"Please search for them. They may prove the crime. In the meantime, we wait to see if we can find the man. I waited to tell you this in hopes of good news. So far, we have none.

"But there's more, Liv. You have to know that when the broker disappeared, I didn't think any more of it. I should have. The funds remained available should he have decided to collect them, but he never did. More than a year later, my London man of business wrote to me that the former owner of Emley had died. By his own hand."

Killian pursed his lips, his heartache palpable. "I felt his loss keenly. I shared the news with my wife who told me my greed was the man's sorrow. She was furious with me. I was shaken. How could I know a man would do such a thing? Could sink so low? But then, of course I did understand poverty. No coin for bread or peat or ale. But my own criticism was small compared to Aileen's. My wife told me how unprincipled I was becoming and gave me an ultimatum. I was to become more ethical or she'd leave me and take our children with her. You can't imagine how that gutted me. She was the love of my life. The one who brought me everything I value, her love, children, a good home, and I couldn't bear to lose her."

He sighed. "Of course, she was right. I changed. I learned to build prosperity for those who work for me and I studied pricing to pay fairly for anything I bought. Occasionally, recognizing the potential of a product or a business, I paid more. I still do."

"I've heard that's true."

"But you've paid a price for my greed," he said with anguish. "If I could change that, I would."

"Much as I wish it, I don't need that. I've come to terms with my past and learned from it. Changed. For the better, I believe."

"I'm pleased to hear it. But I will tell you one thing I've learned. To go to America is to leave your past behind and to work for a better life. But to become an American is to believe you can become a better person."

That filled her with hope. "There is only one way to ameliorate the past. If you can forgive yourself, it is the best beginning. And then there is this." She fished from her skirt pocket the gold ring he'd offered her that day in Paris.

His face fell. "You're giving it back to me?"

"I saved it," she said and put it in his hand, curling his fingers over it. "Frankly, I had no idea what to do with it. At first, that is."

"You can't forgive me," he said it like a death sentence.

Tears pooled on her lashes. "I hoped you might offer it to me again."

His silver eyes glistened with his own tears. "You want me to ask you to marry me?"

"I hoped you would. I could ask you, of course, if you'd excuse the impropriety of it. Whichever you choose, I don't care. I want it done. Above all, I believe the best way to forgive the past may well be to live a future filled with proper loving care for each other."

He shook his head. "Liv, this is extraordinary."

She knew his hesitancy had everything to do with what she had not yet said. "What you were affected us all. But that was yesterday. You and I could choose to live apart, reflecting on those dark days until we die, but what real happiness might that bring either of us?"

She cupped his jaw. "We've both changed. You are richer

but wiser. I am stronger and I hope wise enough to forgive the past. My darling, I love you. I love you as you've become. So if you'll be good enough to ask me once more to marry you, I'd like to accept."

He took the ring and slid it onto her finger. "To wear down the rough edges of each of our personalities."

"To become better people."

"Marry me, please, Liv."

Her heart filled with all the possibilities their lives together held. "I will."

"Say that again."

She laughed and hugged him. "I will. I love you. Now do you mind, dear sir, if I kiss you?"

"Here?" His eyes danced. "In front of all these people?"

"In front of anyone, everyone, everywhere, Killian. I don't care who sees that I love you."

He swung her up and around in his arms. Then he stopped and caught her face between his large warm hands and his lips were on hers, a promise of a magnificent future. "I love you."

EPILOGUE

May 29, 1880
Brighton

L iv grinned to herself as she rounded the drive up
the hill to the house. Open now three months, the
residence was not yet completely furnished, not
fully decorated with all of Killian's prized original paintings,
but the rays of the sun glinting off the pale Mansard roof and
the Bath stone filled her with more than pride in her own
work. It brought tears to her eyes and inspired her with gratitude that her life had been so changed by the love of a man
she once thought she hated.

They'd married last September in London in the American embassy and later in a private church ceremony. To
marry them, the American ambassador required Killian's
birth certificate. But Killian, an immigrant to America at age
six, could show no such paper. He'd certified who he claimed
to be with a few other documents such as London bank state-
ments. With those impressive references, the clergy had no

problems officiating. A day later, the private church ceremony with only family in attendance was to declare they were man and wife for the certitude of everyone in Britain.

Their engagement appeared in the London newspapers and in others. Yet no one had written to her nor had anyone commented that Olivia Louise Emley Bereston was to marry the man who had ruined her father's and her family's lives. Killian had let it be known in his own business circles that the Liverpool broker was a hunted man. Gossipers did the rest to connect the reasons why the American tycoon, Hanniford, would seek out the shipping broker. Once that was public knowledge, others searched for him as well. It seemed the man had committed similar cases of fraud. The Rothschild bank had traced him to Naples and on to Tangier. But once more he had disappeared. The search continued.

However Liv did not need that man's presence to wash away the bitterness of yesterday. She had the love of the first man in her life whom she adored. Marriage to David had been one of mutual convenience, hers for financial succor, his to hide his desires for other men. Marriage to Killian Hanniford was one of fascination and the most thrilling passion she'd ever known. At her age, to find herself abed with her lover at nine or ten in the mornings should be outrageous. She couldn't care at any of that. This was her house, her lover, her husband and she found him more irresistible each time he took her in his arms and told her he adored her.

She giggled at the very thought. But the coach drew nigh to the entrance and she cleared her throat, straightened in the plush black leather squabs and told herself to behave. She had marvelous news to tell, but she must not look like she'd just swallowed a canary. Killian would detect her secret and she wanted to shock him. Shock him to the same kind of giddiness she felt.

Taking the hand of their footman, she allowed him to assist her down the steps of their brougham onto the graveled drive under the *porte cochère*. The May day was a brilliant clear blue with warm breezes off the coast and Hanniford Manor glimmered in the spring sunshine. The wind took tendrils of her hair and coiled them about her face and she smiled that the day was bringing her more than she'd originally anticipated.

"Thank you, Alfred," she said to the young man whom they'd recently hired to live here and assist the new butler. Killian wished to live here in the spring and summer months, keeping his rented Piccadilly house open for his frequent trips to London on business. "Where is Mister Hanniford?"

"His office, Madam. He says he has news and he wishes to see you immediately."

"Wonderful," she said as she strode through the broad front door.

"Jenkins," she greeted the new butler, a young man from Hove who seemed always chipper. "Thank you. You may have my hat and gloves. Has everyone had luncheon?"

"They have, ma'am. As you instructed, we didn't wait for you to return."

"Good." The new Hanniford Manor was chock full to the rafters with Hannifords, young and older and extended family. Remy and Marianne were here with their one-year-old Rand while Marianne finished painting a mural upon one wall in the dining room. Pierce had come down from London two days ago, licking his wounds over the loss of an investment. Ada had arrived last week, "thoroughly distressed over the Season and lack of new amusing men." Lily and Julian had come down from Willowreach yesterday with Garrett along, "in need of cheering up" because Elanna and Carbury were driving them mad with their frequent arguments.

She walked into the spacious foyer and turned left. Before her along the straight line to the terrace, stood the Dominican arches, the sea and the serenity of this life she was building with a man she cherished.

Near the end of the hall, she stopped and knocked on the wooden door.

Killian's rich bass voice reached out to her and she entered.

"Hello!" He removed his spectacles, pushed up and grinned at her. His hair bore more silver strands at his temples. He might even be developing a waving silver streak over his brow. "How are you?"

"Very well," she said, the news bubbling inside her like a hot spring.

"The plasterers at the Lockern site are getting along, are they?" He came around his desk to take her in his arms, hold her close to his strong body and kiss her on the lips.

"They are. They see the value of working with another crew. Finally."

"Ah, well. When you pay them all well, who can complain, eh?"

"True."

He pulled back to peer at her. "What?"

"What do you mean? I fixed the labor dispute. We are all back to work."

"You look..." His brow furrowed. "Different."

"Really?" How to hide things from a man who saw everything about you? Your desire for him, your never-ending need to crawl into his arms at night and to kiss him until he caressed each inch of your own body?

"Your hair. It's mussed from the wind."

She patted it. Ready to tell him.

"Now, I have two things to show you." He took her hand and led her toward the drawing room.

There, against the vermilion walls, framed by fresh flowers in huge vases, he'd hung the portrait by Delacroix of Chopin. Playing the man's compositions as she did often when they were in their London house in Piccadilly, she laughed when Killian had told her he owned the piece. "Even if it's only half of the original."

"Half? Why?" she'd asked, shocked.

"No idea. Some ass cut the canvas and here is Chopin by himself. Alone. Poor bugger."

But today, Chopin looked very different.

Or beneath his portrait, standing boldly forth in the north corner near the large stone fireplace was a new element. A huge black grand piano.

She halted in her tracks. "Killian."

"It arrived while you were out." He led her to the marvelous piece and offered her the long bench. "Will you sit? You look like you should, darling."

"Killian. Oh, my. A concert grand piano? For the country?"

"Do you like it?"

"Oh, Killian. I'd be quite insane not to adore it." She ran her hands over satin finish and the golden inscription of the manufacturer's name. "By Blüthner? You had this shipped from Leipzig?"

"I ordered it from their agent in Cavendish Square. You read that Richard Strauss owns one. I think you need one, too. Besides, I want to hear you play often. When you come in from work on your houses. When you're happy. In the afternoons, as you did last year when you filled Willowreach with calm and joy."

She spun and rushed into his arms. And kissed him, kissed him, kissed him. "There's been so much to do, I'd forgotten how I miss it. How I love it."

"I want you to enjoy every minute here," he said as he grinned at her.

"How could I not? I'm with you. You are my every dream come true."

"As you are mine, my darling." He pulled away, a devilish grin flowing over his features, and took her wrist again. "Come now. There's more."

"More? More what? Where are we going? I have to talk to you."

"Soon. Come along, Mrs. Hanniford. You will love this news."

"I liked this last bit."

"This one's different. Old. Rare."

"You're being mysterious, Hanniford."

"I know." He led her from the drawing room down the hall and out past the orangeries to the terrace. "Stand here. Close your eyes."

She did as she was told. The breezes off the shores wafted through her hair and refreshed her face. "Ready."

"You remember the Dominicans?"

"Of course."

"And the Templars?"

"I do."

"Hmmm. Well, then. I saw old man Dunwoody today."

"All right." When Killian had purchased the land, he had Carruthers tell the old fisherman that he would not be dispossessed of his home. In fact, Killian had arranged it with the land agent that the plot on which Dunwoody's cottage stood was his, free and clear in perpetuity. They saw him each morning as he walked the beach. A happy man because Killian had made him so. "And what? Have you given him something more?"

"No. He came up to talk soon after you took the carriage down to town. And he has given us a gift."

"Wonderful! I like gifts. What is it and can I open my eyes now please?"

"I know you do. And yes, you can look at this."

Killian stood before her with his palms up, hands open. Nestled in each was one gold coin. Their edges frayed, the inscriptions ragged, they looked ancient.

"Dear heavens." She breathed. "You don't think that they're...?"

He gave her a lopsided grin. "I do."

"Noooo." She put a fingertip to the inscriptions and leaned over to try to read them. "Old French?"

His long dark brows shot high. "Your guess is better than mine."

"How did he find them? Where?"

"When they leveled the land over there at the eastern edge of the cliff, the landscapers moved tons of earth. Dunwoody said he walked the beach one morning last week, and saw a glint in the sun. He went to investigate and here are two of twenty-five gold florins. Or, as he would say modestly, we think they are."

Liv threw back her head to laugh and clap her hands. "Dear me. We must have them appraised. Take them to London. An expert in the British Museum. A medievalist, don't you think? Or a lecturer at Oxford or...or...someone!" She hugged him. "This is marvelous. And just what we need."

"We do?" He threw her a frown laced with a smile.

"We do. Have you told anyone else?"

"No, only you. You deserved to hear it first."

"I did. Why?"

"Because you've brought me this treasure."

"No, I didn't. Dunwoody did!" She chuckled.

"I say you did. You forgave me."

"As you did me," she said with assurance.

Killian wrapped her in arms and kissed her with a big

smack on the lips. "You bring me treasure every day you smile at me and kiss me and make love to me."

She giggled. "I do believe you're right!"

He snorted in laughter. "Humility thy name is woman!"

"You encourage me in such silliness. Now," she said with firmness, "you must be quiet and let me talk to you. I have news for you."

"What?"

"Put those coins in your pockets and look at me."

He jerked back an inch. "What? You look alternately like you will die laughing or you'll swallow a pigeon whole."

She strolled away from him, collecting her giddiness like golden coins for a horde of happiness.

"What is it?" He followed her to the edge of the wall. "You have another commission? Camille is coming down from that new school? She hates this one as much as that last one we sent her to and—"

"No." She was chuckling as she turned to him in the sunlight and saw that she had terrified him.

He captured her face between his hands. His gaze was dark with dread, his body rigid. "Don't do this to me. To yourself. You've not been well. I know it. You won't talk about it and I've let you have your time to decipher what it is. Now I'm not waiting any longer. Tell me. You went to a doctor, didn't you?"

Damn. This man could outwit her at the drop of a hat. "No."

"No?" He sagged. He hauled her into the vise of his arms, his lips buried against her ear. "What then?"

"I went to consult a midwife. A woman I met when I lived up on the Parade." She pulled away to view him as he dropped his jaw. "My darling husband, I'm so glad we have this very large house. You see, we're going to fill it up. I am expecting a baby."

Shock turned him white. Then he threw back his head to laugh and capture her up in his arms. With tears in his eyes, he smiled at her. "A child of forgiveness."

"A child of love."

THE END

Who is Cerise DeLand?

Cerise DeLand loves to write about dashing heroes and the sassy women they adore. Whether she's penning historical romances or contemporaries, she has received praise for her poetic elegance and accuracy of detail.

An award-winning author of more than 50 novels, she's been published since 1991 by Pocket Books, St. Martin's Press, Kensington and independent presses. Her books have been monthly selections of the Doubleday Book Club and the Mystery Guild. Plus she's won nominations and awards for Best Historical of the Year, Best Regency and scores of rave reviews from *Romantic Times, Affair de Coeur, Publisher's Weekly* and more.

To research, she's dived into the oldest texts and dustiest library shelves. She's also traveled abroad, trusty notebook and pen in hand, to visit the chateaux and country homes she loves to people with her own imaginary characters.

And at home every day? She loves to cook, hates to dust, goes swimming at least once a week and tries (desperately) to grow vegetables in her arid backyard in south Texas!

www.cerisedeland.com
cerise.deland@gmail.com

Contemporaries

Tall, Hard and Trouble, box set

Tall, Hard and Mine, box set,

Coming Soon!

Tall, Hard and Fierce, box set,

Coming Soon!

***

Sign up for Cerise's newsletter:

Cherries and Bon Bons http://eepurl.com/Jm55L

www.ingramcontent.com/pod-product-compliance
Lightning Source LLC
Chambersburg PA
CBHW060429180626
46817CB00007B/2737